As If She Had a Say

As If She Had a Say

stories

Jennifer Fliss

Curbstone Books / Northwestern University Press
Evanston, Illinois

Curbstone Books
Northwestern University Press
www.nupress.northwestern.edu

This is a work of fiction. Names, characters, places, and incidents either
are the product of the author's imagination or are used fictitiously,
and any resemblance to actual persons, living or dead, business
establishments, events, or locales is entirely coincidental.

Printed in the United States of America

10 9 8 7 6 5 4 3 2 1

Library of Congress Cataloging-in-Publication Data

Names: Fliss, Jennifer, author.
Title: As if she had a say : stories / Jennifer Fliss.
Description: Evanston, Illinois : Curbstone Books/Northwestern
     University Press, 2023.
Identifiers: LCCN 2023002278| ISBN 9780810146259 (paperback)|
     ISBN 9780810146266 (ebook)
Subjects: LCSH: Women—Fiction.| LCGFT: Short stories.
Classification: LCC PS3606.L573 A9 2023| DDC 813.6—dc23/eng/20230118
LC record available at https://lccn.loc.gov/2023002278

Contents

As She Melted

What is your gender? Check one:

☐ man

☐ woman

☐ nonbinary

As she melted, Marla wondered about the debris under the refrigerator. Why had she never cleaned that? She noticed a moldy nub of unrecognizable food. Something that might've once been part of one of the three-course meals she dutifully fed her husband each night, but what it was now, she couldn't say. Her fingers and toes were already gone, having dripped off moments before.

She saw that she had not fed the cat that day; she could hear Jester howling, but since she was turning into liquid, there wasn't much to be done about that. Her palms were going now, rivulets of her collecting in pools on the floor. It started earlier, her fingernails moving about as she tried to paint them.

What is the name of the polish?

☐ I'm Not Really a Waitress

☐ Chick Flick Cherry

☐ Lost My Bikini on Molokini

Marla thought maybe she was having a stroke. When she was bringing in the mail, her fingerprints began to circle, like tiny whirlpools, and the mail fell to the ground. She left it and ran inside. Maybe she would discuss it with her husband when he came home from work. But now she couldn't move and stood, liquefying, beside the kitchen island under a canopy of pots and pans.

She should warn Brent. She didn't want him to slip and he didn't like surprises. Marla felt her hands fully dissolve. The watch Brent bought her for her birthday dangled from her wrist and then clattered to the floor. *Since you can't seem to keep track of anything,* he had said, and thrown the box at her. *Tossed,* he clarified later as he dabbed the blood from her forehead where the box glanced. It was a Chopard, loose tiny diamonds skittered around the face of it, expensive tears.

She heard the deep thrum of the car pulling into the driveway. *Thwack,* the door slammed. The jangle of keys. And then, nothing.

"Brent?" Her arms to the elbows had softened, and she continued to drip. A stream of her moved toward the stairs and out into the dining room. She was barely visible, the whole of her already semitransparent. She felt a slight tide pull through her, in and out. In and out. What could once have been called breath was something more fluid now—something that might dissipate at any moment.

The door opened.

What is the first thing Brent says?

☐ "Marla!? Marla, what the fuck? The mail was all over the
driveway."

☐ "Oh my god. What's going on?"

☐ "You'll never guess what that slut Marie in HR did today."

Marla wished and did not wish for him to make his way to the
kitchen. He took his shoes off—brogues—then his jacket—navy
pea coat—and put his work badge and keys in a bowl on the front
table. She knew these things, a routine she dreaded since what
followed was often the awkwardly staged play of dinner, that
modern domestic tragedy.

"What the fuck, Marla?" he said.

"It seems I'm melting," she said.

"You're making a mess," he said.

"Yes, that's true," she said. He went to the kitchen sink and,
from the cabinet beneath it, procured a small bucket. In his
argyle socks, he stepped in her.

"Really?" He looked at her, her face softening, his hardening. "My socks. Now my socks are wet." He placed the bucket
under one dripping arm. From the counter, he took a stockpot
and placed it under her other arm. *Ping, ping, ping* . . . until the
pinging turned into the hollow sound of water hitting water, and
then *splash, splash, splash*—the sound of her spilling out of the
containers. She would not be contained. Not by him.

"Brent, I'm melting. I am turning into water and I am very
sorry about your socks, but do you think—"

He picked up the watch. "I don't have insurance on this."
The glass had grown cloudy with moisture. "Marla, there is
so much I do for you. Isn't that right?" He peeled off his socks,
tossed them on the counter next to the salad she'd been making.

Grabbed a fistful of dried cranberries and pushed them into his mouth.

Yes, Brent did so much for her.

What are some of the things Brent did for Marla?

☐ He pinched her hips when there was something to pinch.

☐ He fucked her even when she got fat.

☐ He went on trips to Vietnam and Paris and Vegas.

☐ He worked all day, working long hours into the night and taking black town cars home.

☐ He confessed to his myriad affairs.

☐ All of the above.

At least I'm honest, he always said.

Brent folded up the cuffs of his trousers, waded into her nascent lagoon, and kissed her. Hard. His vile effluent flowed past her tongue, down her throat, into her intestines, and then splashed to the ground; she had already succumbed to liquidity below her belly button.

"That's disgusting, Marla," he said, and he moved toward the refrigerator. Opened. Grabbed a beer. Closed.

Marla's pants and underwear were crumpled in a pile beneath her. She wondered: *When would this be done with?* It didn't hurt, which surprised her. It felt as if someone were running their kneading palms into her body, soothing her, removing her knots, her anxieties. It was the kind of pain one associated with relaxation, a great massage at a day spa. She shimmied off the rest of her clothes so she could watch what happened next.

"You'll clean that up when you're done," Brent said and left her there, melting into the radiant heated bamboo floors. The cat lapped her up, too ineffectual to stop the flood, but Marla appreciated the gesture. She heard the television go on in the other room. And then the phone rang. It rang and rang and rang.

"I can't get that, Brent," she hollered into the other room. Begrudgingly—she could hear it in his voice—he answered.

"Yeah? Hey, Carl." There was some silence; presumably, Carl was speaking. Carl lived next door and the two lawyers had bonded over a love of making money and dirty jokes, often at the expense of their wives—this Marla knew, as they didn't even try to hide it from her.

"Yeah, okay. See you in five," Brent said and hung up. "Hon, I'm going out. Hit up the Deuce and Eagle with Carl. He's having issues with Debra again." At this point Marla was water up to her breasts. Was this what it was like to be a mermaid? Brent came back into the kitchen.

"Brent, I don't think this is reversible," Marla said.

"That *is* so weird, but you know . . . I've seen weirder," he said. He got close, stared into her eyes, didn't move for a while. A modern Narcissus.

"It just kind of . . . started happening. I didn't do anything," she said.

"I mean, Carl said something about Debra being all wet, but I just assumed . . . well . . . you know. I wonder if it's all you women?"

"What should we do?" Marla asked.

"I don't know. I mean, I'm really hungry right now." He nodded to the partially made dinner on the counter. "So I was just gonna go, you know, meet up with Carl. We can talk about this later."

He left. The mermaid woman who was not a mermaid, and who was now only a face, swelled and released, burst like a storm cloud.

An angry torrent of Marla and of Debra and of each woman who lived on the cul-de-sac, of every woman in the town and the state and on and on, gushed forth. The mothers, the wives, the women who lived alone. A tidal wave, they tossed aside cars and trucks and upended playground structures and stop signs. They inundated buildings and cities and villages and, as they drowned, the men coughed and sputtered. They choked on their women, wondering.

What did they wonder?

☐ Where are our wives, leaving us here at this moment, in this squall?

☐ Fuck, my balls; it's cold.

☐ What about Madeline and Holly and Candace? And that girl from the café? What was her name?

☐ Was this what global warming was all about? Mother Nature's such a bitch.

☐ Dear God, can you hear me? I'm sorry I . . .

☐ So, this is it?

And the women filled the streets and empty pools, the culverts and valleys, with their fear and love and remorse and hope and sorrow and bitterness. If the men listened hard enough, they'd understand that if they'd just put the cork back in the drain, they could've all been saved.

The Cresting Water

"Ma'am, you're gonna need to leave the premises," the man at the door—a boy, really—is saying while the storm begins its assaults. The wind whips around the small Cape Cod cottage. Rain pelts the boy; the storm is growing.

"No, it's okay, son, I'll be fine," Mildred says as she returns to the kitchen sink and wipes her mug dry. She makes sure she gets every last drop of water before placing it in the rusty drying rack. The mug reads "Elderica House, a Place for You" in generic white cursive. Also in the drying rack is a single wineglass, speckled with water spots but clean. She motions for the young man to step inside. The house smells of burnt coffee with the vaguely herbal notes of a vapor rub.

"What's your name, son?"

"Steve," he answers as he closes the door behind him, loose leaves and rogue raindrops following and settling on the laminate. His hair is scraggly and his bright orange safety vest exaggerates the redness of his acne. Beneath the ruddiness, the boy's chin is barely present and his eyes are runny and small, but his cheekbones are high and friendly. He looks like Walter.

"You look hungry. Are you hungry, Steve? Why don't you have a seat." Mildred points to a chair at the kitchen table and pulls a triangular chocolate bar from a drawer.

"Ma'am, I can't. We have to evacuate the area. The storm is real close. A surge is expected. This whole area could be under water in . . . uh . . . I don't know . . . real soon."

"I know the dangers of the area, son. We've had storms. We've had flooding," Mildred scolds. "You've still got some time yet."

"I'm not sure about that. I don't . . . I, um . . ." Steve stammers.

"Have a seat." She points again with a wooden spoon. "I won't keep you long."

"Ma'am, I've got orders to—"

"Sit!" He sits. She brings him a mug of coffee—this one reading "World's Best Aunt"—that she has just brewed. She pours some for herself in the newly cleaned retirement-home mug. The shutters awaken, thrashing the clapboard house. Steve stands, alarmed.

"Oh, that happens if it even *thinks* about raining," she says. "Walter was supposed to hammer them back in. Toblerone?"

"Walter?" Steve asks. "Your son?"

"No. Not my son," she says, choosing to leave the question in the air. "So, Steve, you're married." It was not a question; Mildred nods to his hand, where a thin gold wedding band clutches his finger. She breaks off a triangle of chocolate and hands it to him. She no longer wears her own ring.

"A year and a half," he says.

"A year and a half," she repeats.

"Actually, one year, eight months, four days," he corrects.

"Well, *that* is a marriage still in its infancy. I just love this chocolate. It used to be harder to find. When Walter and I would go up to Canada we'd stock up," she says and motions to the yellow bag on the counter. She joins Steve at the table. The lights flicker, threatening to go out.

"I've got a generator," she says. "Now tell me about your bride."

"We really have to go," Steve says, starting to edge his chair back.

"Is there any flooding yet?" Mildred asks, pointing outside.

"No, but—"

"There's still time then."

"Well, I guess just a minute or two."

"Go on then," Mildred says, as she takes a seat and bites into the chocolate. "Your wife."

"I, uh, I'm married to her. I love her. Obviously."

"Obviously," Mildred repeats. "And?"

"And, uh . . . there's Carina. That's our little girl."

"Pretty name," Mildred says.

"It means caring," Steve says, turning the band on his finger. It comes off easily and he rolls it around his fingers.

"You love your baby so much, don't you? How about your wife?" Mildred asks.

"Well, uh. She's really nice."

"Nice. Nice!? Young man. Those lilies are *nice*," she says, gesturing toward a vase. "What's wrong then?"

"Nothing."

"Pardon my language, but, like hell," Mildred chirps.

"It's just hard on her. Y'know. The baby keeps her awake and I . . . I have this job that keeps me gone all the time. It's new, y'know?" he says.

"New?"

"My job. It's only my third week. Kind of crazy, right? That this big storm comes around." Outside, the rain hammers the

siding and the roof, quickly ping pinging, like bullets. The lights
falter again.

Steve thrusts his seat back. "Come on. This just isn't safe. You
know it's not. Let's go," he says and starts to gets up. "Ma'am—"

"Mildred," she corrects, and places her hand on his knee,
keeping him at the table. She nudges his cup of coffee, encouraging him to drink, plying him with chocolate.

"Mildred, I'm sorry, but I am supposed to get you and everyone else out of their houses. It's . . . like, you know, my first
big . . . event. And everyone else already left."

"The Shiffs next door?" Mildred asks.

"Green house?"

"Mhm."

"Yeah, they left."

"Wisners?" she asks.

"Which house?"

"Brick one across the way. Newlyweds, you know. Everyone's
got their problems, son," Mildred says.

"Yes, they're gone, too. Mildred, you're the only one left on
the block. Maybe in the whole neighborhood. It's just you. By
yourself. You're not safe."

"Steve. I have no intention of leaving. You go right on ahead
without me. Tell your boss I wasn't here. Here, take this." She
hands him a full chocolate bar from her drawer stash. "It'll be a
long night. You'll get hungry. And finish your coffee. I hope you
don't mind me saying, but it looks like you could use it." Steve
sips and winces.

"I know. Most people don't like it. What I really liked was
Chock Full o' Nuts. Remember?"

"I—"

"No, no. Of course you don't. You're just a young thing. You could be my grandson."

"Where are they? Your grandkids?"

"Oh, it was just me and Walter. Steve, I'm not going with you. I told you that. You should go on now," Mildred says, and goes to the sink. The shutters grow more aggressive. "Go on to your wife and daughter."

"Ma'am. Mildred. I won't leave without you."

"How much time do you think we have?" she asks.

"Not sure. Hour? Half hour? Maybe less. I don't really know," Steve guesses.

Mildred thinks for a moment. "Oh! We're still good for a while. Like the storm back in '85. Everyone was a fright but it turned out just fine. Evacuated the whole town for nothing. But I'll be quick so you can go on with your work."

"I told you I won't—"

"Then maybe I'll go with you. All right?"

Sheets of water drive against the glass. The twitching shadows of trees maraud against the floor in the dim light. The wind howls at the door, huffing and puffing. Inside, it's warm and calm.

Steve thinks about it. "Okay," he mutters.

"Do you swim, Steve?"

"Yeah, sure."

"I never liked to swim. Never learned. Was too scared as a child when my pa wanted to give me lessons. Nicholas and Warren—those were my brothers—they took to water like fish. Scaly, slimy creatures, they were. Not me. I just sat with my mother helping her knit or reading books all those summers on the beach. Didn't bother me none. But there I am, seventy years old and Walter—fully aware of my, well . . . my . . . phobia—

surprises me for my birthday with a bottle of pinot grigio and a rowboat!"

The whipping shutters intensify, striking in cadence with the steadily falling rain. A wail from an ambulance or fire truck in the distance cries out.

"It's getting worse. Listen to that," Steve says.

"Oh, just another minute." She reaches for his mug and takes it to the sink. Then Steve is behind her and carefully takes her elbow.

"Come on, Mildred. Let's go," he says. But she shakes him off. Reaches for another chocolate. Unwraps it. Hands him half.

"There it was. The man I'd been with for nearly fifty years making a present of my worst fear. 'No way,' I told him. 'Worst present ever,' I said—and let me tell you this, Steve, Walter was very good at giving utterly ridiculous gifts. He once got me some hard-to-find replacement bobbin for a sewing machine. I have never owned a sewing machine in my life! Valentine's Day after Valentine's Day of romance novels. Hate 'em. Give me a mystery or thriller any day. And those covers! Eventually, it became a joke between us. Here, let me show you something." Mildred leads Steve into the hallway, near the stairs. At least thirty small wooden frames line the walls in neat rows. There are so many they sweep down the hall and up to the second floor landing. Each frame is filled with a romance cover: shiny half-dressed men with long blond hair and obscene muscles stroke women with robust cleavage underneath titles like *Her Rocky Mountain Protector*, *Champagne for Charlotte*, and *Love and Other Cures*.

"Now, this is something you miss out on with all those electronic books!" Mildred laughs.

"Okay, that's something I haven't ever seen before, but—" Steve says. Just then, the lights give a final shudder and the power goes out with an electric gasp. "That means it's time to go," Steve says. "Are you ready?" He reaches out for Mildred, grasping at air. The wind bellows. The rain pounds. In the dark, the sounds of the storm are almost soothing.

"Oh, Steve, I told you I was going to stay. You go on." Her voice has moved farther away, back toward the kitchen.

"But you said—"

"I know. I'm sorry. I simply can't. Please pardon an old lady wanting to tell her story. Sometimes, there are stories worth hearing but there aren't people around to listen to them." Mildred feels her way along the wall, following the familiar path, counting the frames with her fingertips.

"Mildred?" Steve calls, but only the storm responds, an intruder at the door. Then, a roar, and the electricity winks back.

"Generator," Mildred says as she greets him in the hallway. She hands him one of the romance novel frames, *The Hardness of Love*. "Here," Mildred says, "one of our favorites." She takes a seat on the bottom step and continues. A thin pond of water is forming on the old wood beneath her feet.

"So, there Walter is. A bottle of wine in one hand, a huge wooden oar in the other, and a stupid grin on his face. 'Surprise!' he yelled. Surprise indeed! Then he went on to explain how much work he'd done to get the boat from Andy Little down the way and the wine is a such-and-such vintage and isn't it a great night, the stars are out, and on and on. It was very sweet. Then, he pulled out a giant Toblerone, one of those king-sized ones. *That* he'd gotten right. He'd gone to so much trouble.

"You know, on summer evenings, we'd sit in the pool out back and snack on our chocolate and Walter would read the stars. Of course, he had no idea what he was talking about. 'That's the Big Dipper,' he'd say and then point to Orion's belt."

"You have a pool? But I thought you didn't—"

"We had it emptied when we bought the house. I told you I *really* don't like water. But it was a big hit with the neighborhood kids, though I'm sure they would've preferred it filled. Anyway, my birthday. Walter looked so proud of himself. So, well, I went ahead and did it. He put the moldy life vest over my head and off we went on the lake. Farther and farther we rowed out. Occasionally, one of those obnoxious powerboat monstrosities whizzed by, setting our little boat, and my heart, into convulsions. My fingers ached from clutching the sides of the boat. I think at that point Walter knew enough not to rock the boat, literally. 'Okay Walter, that was great; now let's go back,' I told him. He just smiled his wicked little smile—he *was* devilishly handsome. He looked a little like you, actually. All shaggy hair and squinty eyes. He said he had a surprise. As if this adventure wasn't enough of a surprise!

"Then we could hear the motor of another one of those bully boats nearing. I braced myself. It was getting closer. Closer than any of the others before it. Closer and then closer and before I could even see it, our boat went under and I was tossed out. Oh! I have never been so scared in my life. I went under briefly, only long enough to think I would never surface. But then I was buoyed up by my vest. That stinking life vest. The stinking life vest that Walter put on me. I knew that Walter didn't swim too well himself. To waste the life vest on me, when he was just as useless in the water."

Steve's walkie-talkie crackles to life with admonishments and orders, spit through the electronic waves. He lowers the volume. Steve leans in to hear Mildred through the storm battering the house.

"I floundered around a little, then stopped. I floated there, calling for Walter. Finally, I heard him. 'Marco!' is what he was shouting. Can you believe it? I returned with 'Polo!' thinking he would draw nearer. Until I couldn't hear the 'Marco' anymore. I tried and tried to reach him, but I couldn't find him. I finally made my way to the shore and stood, looking for him. If I tried to find a phone, I could've missed him, you understand. I scanned the water. I think I might have seen splashing in the distance, but who knows. I don't know how long I stood there, at the shore. Useless. Then I went wailing up the hill to the nearby restaurant to call 911. Of course, it was too late.

"So, I was ready for this, Steve. You understand? I was planning on it," Mildred says into the darkening room. It seemed the generator was losing power. "This time, I can save him," she says, looking out a window. The wind whistles through a crack between the window and the sill. A crash comes from the other room, glass breaks.

"I'm so sorry," Steve says.

"I am ready to go now. I didn't know where or when. But I knew—" Mildred trails off. Another window blows out somewhere upstairs. "Now, please," Mildred says as she stands. "Go on." She turns to go upstairs, taking each step deliberately. She knows it will be her last time. The voice in Steve's walkie-talkie grows more insistent. This time, he turns it up.

"All hands must evacuate and meet search and rescue in ten minutes, at nine-oh-five, at the corner of Third and Beach," fizzles the voice.

Steve hollers up the stairs. "Mildred! Please! You promised!"

She turns. "I've made other promises, son."

"Well, I won't go then. I'll stay right here. With you," Steve says.

"You will do no such thing. You will go back to your family. They need you."

"But—"

"I'm an old woman. It's okay."

"Ma'am."

"Mildred."

"Mildred. Please," he says. Mildred nods, and as she walks up the stairs, she wipes each of the frames clear of dust.

"Mildred!" Steve cries. She does not respond, but begins to sing, off-key.

In her bedroom, the wind spilling through a broken window, Mildred pours herself into the bathing suit, its black-brown Lycra stretching at her middle, the V-neck drooping a little low, expressing her wilted cleavage and loose décolletage. She admires the woman in the mirror. Could that really be her? Not the same body she had at twenty, when she'd met Walter. Not even the body she had at seventy. But not bad for eighty-one.

"Oof!" she cries as she steps backward on the carpet, away from the old woman. On tiptoes, she walks to her bed and sits, struggling to access the bottom of her foot. She finally manages and sees the sparkling glint of glass. She takes a deep breath and pulls the shard out. A small thread of blood blooms, and she cradles her foot. She waits. She isn't sure for how long or exactly for what. Glass explodes throughout the house. From the backyard, she hears the rasping sounds of metal being pulled or twisted. *The pool ladder*, she thinks.

After Walter died, Mildred would sit inside the empty pool in the backyard for hours, staring up from the deep well filled with ghosts of pool parties, the tile cooling her back. She'd eat her Toblerone and wonder how, despite being in a pool, she was not, in fact, floating. It was in that empty pool she decided she would join Walter.

Then, she hears it, faint, but distinct, "Marco!"

She walks out of her room, onto the upper landing. The storm encroaches further. The water asserts itself midway up the stairs. It laps at the walls, discoloring the creamy floral wallpaper. Even in the murky dark, the shadow of where the sun bleached the wallpaper around *The Hardness of Love*'s now-empty frame is visible. This is where the water reached, they will say, where the red roses have blushed harder and grown darker. This is how high.

She steps into the water, slowly eases her body into it. It is surprisingly warm. "Polo!" she responds.

"Marco!" She hears the return in the distance, quiet but familiar. She takes her first stroke. The water parts in the web of her fingers easily. It isn't too difficult. It feels pleasant, even, the water wrapping her up, warming her, making her feel protected; womblike. A small whirlpool brews near where the coat rack once stood. She can see two scarfs dancing in the water; her yellow rain jacket is stuck on the doorknob trying to escape.

The rain has stopped but the water keeps rising. Mildred treads, pumping her legs in the metallic-scented water. "I'm coming," she calls into the hypnotic eddy.

As if on cue, the front door splits, the top half detaching and releasing into the water. She watches the current pull the water out and down the street. She takes a gulp as it rushes by. It tastes like gasoline and salt. She makes her way toward the half-open door, pushing her scarves out of the way. This time, I've got you, she thinks.

"Marco!" she hears again. Swimming out into the lawn, which is now several feet beneath her, she sees Steve. He is balancing in a small rowboat—not unlike Andy Little's—tied by thick rope to the light post, its bulb dead. The vessel is lightly tossed about, but he is young and a swimmer and won't have a problem if he becomes untethered. Does he see her? Mildred glides under the water. It is quieter down here. She breaks the surface closer to Steve's boat. He is searching the water with a flashlight. Other than the thin circle of light it creates, everything is dark. He doesn't see her. He picks a limp doll out of the water. He adds it to a pile of bloated pieces of paper, shoes, and books swollen with storm.

"Mildred!" Steve cries at the house.

Mildred treads silently, watching Steve. From the torrent, he scoops up a pale yellow piece of paper. It's a Toblerone wrapper, devoid of its chocolate. He drops it into the pile but then seems to think twice and bends to retrieve it. Stuffing it in his pocket, he looks up at Mildred's house.

"Mildred!" he shouts again, his hands cupping his lips like a bullhorn.

Mildred watches the young man who looks like Walter as he tries desperately to save her. She once again hears "Marco!" but it is growing fainter. Hunger rumbles in her belly. Other than the chocolate and coffee, it has been too long since she had eaten. When had Steve last eaten? Would he go home to his wife and daughter for dinner? Did it matter? Did *he* need saving?

Mildred knows she doesn't have much longer. The water is smooth but the current is quick. Her nose is dripping and the cold seeps into her bones. She hears Walter call again. It is such a lovely voice and my, how she's missed it. *I'm coming*, Mildred thinks, and she makes a decision. Walter will be there when she is ready, and then they will have forever to laugh and eat their chocolate and talk about the time in the storm that almost was but wasn't. Amid the roiling water and the debris, Mildred calls out. Steve looks up, his face drenched in relief as he unties his boat, paddles through the mire, and rescues her.

Splintered

While laughing over something the neighbor says, Katie slaps an old picnic table. This is the first splinter. It embeds itself quickly, inserting itself readily, as if her skin were dough. She squeals at the intrusion and Josh insists on using a needle to get it out. They fill the small bathroom with their two bodies. Beneath Katie's feet, the tile is cool, but still she sweats. Josh, too; she can see it on the sides of his face and in the darkened patches of his T-shirt. He closes one eye and scrape, scrape, digs. It's not a needle but a safety pin. He hasn't sterilized it, but surely it doesn't matter, he tells Katie. She struggles not to pull her hand back from his and he squeezes her pinky as he works. He is not successful, and Katie sucks her finger the rest of the day between bites of Greek salad and taco dip.

The next day, Katie holds tight to the railing as she ascends the steep steps to the back door. There is a piercing into the delicate flesh between thumb and forefinger. She gasps; usually, splinters don't hurt so much. This is the second splinter.

The ladder from the garage. A half-done birdhouse. The deck she's been meaning to clean up. The third, fourth, and fifth splinters. Josh says maybe she has particularly tender flesh. His eyes shimmer as he says it, looking almost like they are filling with water, but Katie knows better. She doesn't feel like having sex but doesn't say so. While Josh is in her, steadily moving his body over hers, Katie studies the most recent splinter near her thumb. It seems large and should be easy to dislodge. She will try later with tweezers.

The house is cold. Katie is always cold, no matter the season; once the dusk sets in and the house takes on colors only visible during those few minutes a day, she arranges the wood in the fireplace to set a fire. She cries out. Six.

"You okay?" Josh shouts from the kitchen. He is making dinner. She hates salmon, but he insists it's healthy for her.

"Fine," she says.

"You want me to do that? I can set the fire."

"So can I."

"I usually set the fires," he says. It sounds like he is eating something, mouth filled with masticated things.

"I know," Katie says, and flips the vent switch.

It is not as if she decides to leave the foreign objects there, embedded in her skin. But no amount of coaxing seems to work them out. She scrapes along her surface, skin flaking, her own self dropping like snow. She tries tweezers and needles, sucking and fingernails. She remembers something her father told her when she was young: if you don't take splinters out, they stay forever. They become a part of you. Her father wanted to abrade her skin. You might have to get amputated, he'd said. Cut it off completely or it will become infected. He had come at her with a sharp object, its tip and his eyes glinting. She had envisioned her skin gradually losing its softness, hardening, turning to bark. Her imagination took her further and further until she was a tree in a field, rooted, unable to move, birds flitting through her branches, sap running down her middle. Anyway, her father was a beast. He would not even allow her to climb her own trunk.

It should be said that Katie works with wood, something she never dreamed she'd do as an adult. She'd been recused from the woodshed in summer camp after ineptitude with a vise. She hadn't even gotten to saws. But now, she makes birdhouses and dollhouses and small tables, sometimes carving out small necklaces like puzzle pieces. She sells these wares at local craft fairs, one time venturing as far as Portland, three hours south. She attempted an online store, but found the intricacies of e-commerce daunting. And she likes meeting her customers, knowing that what she creates with her hands will become a part of their homes, their lives.

She is packing some recently made items into plastic storage containers. Today she has rented a stall at the local flea and farmers' market. She will put up colorful bunting that reads *Katie's Kwality Wood*. She hates the name; Josh came up with it, and in a fit of productivity had made all her collateral with these words. She has a stack of business cards—matte, not glossy. She's made little slabs of wood which will act as display shelves. The shelves go into boxes along with mini plastic bags for jewelry, a cash box, a credit card reader, five birdhouses, two dollhouses, and three small stools with paisley designs carved into them. She has a few brochures that say she can build custom items: stools with children's names in them, wedding decor, cutting boards. She can bend wood, but this isn't easy and she doesn't do it often.

She hugs Josh; she is that excited. He smells like hotel soap.

"That smell's making me nauseous," she says.

"Nauseated."

"You, too?" she asks.

"No, it's nauseated."

"Whatever. Your new soap or new cologne or whatever is making me sick."

"Bitch," he says, then waits ten seconds before he smiles and punches her shoulder like it's a joke.

"Okay, I'm going," Katie says.

"Where to?"

"The market. Remember, I told you," she says, filling the car's trunk.

"We have the party at Andy and Marie's today," Josh says.

"Well, I can't go. This has been on the calendar for—"

"Fuck the calendar," he says. She looks up at his eyes. They are dark and he goes to stand in front of the car, blocking her way out.

"Josh."

"It's Andy's fortieth."

"Tell them I'm sorry."

"You tell them."

"Josh, I'm going to be late. I have to set up." He puts his hands on his hips and she imagines that this is what he looked like as a belligerent five-year-old. She had hoped to have a child of her own one day. But she is thirty-nine, not too late but getting there. When they were dating, Josh said he wanted kids, too, a whole brood of them. He has said little about it in recent years.

Katie gets into her car and starts the ignition. Through the bug-spattered windshield Josh looks like he wants to be a super-hero, as if he is waiting for someone to save. Arms still on his hips, head cocked slightly upward. One of her splinters begins to pulse. Mostly, they do not cause her pain after they lodge into her body, but they stay put, none of them giving up, not one allowing her to pry it free.

She revs the engine and Josh smirks. She rolls down her window. "Josh, move!"

He doesn't say anything. Doesn't budge. She can see Philip from across the street, eighty-nine (he tells everyone) and nosy, kind and widowed. He is standing in his driveway no longer occupied by a vehicle, watching the scene unfolding in Katie and Josh's yard.

Katie revs again. "I'll come later," she shouts. "I'll meet you there, okay?" She won't. She has the stall until the end of the market, which is at six o'clock. She will come home, take a bath, and calculate her revenue for the day, determine if it was a loss or not given the time she put into it. Either way, she will have alone time. That is valuable.

She allows the car to jerk forward a foot or two. It works and Josh jumps out of the way into the long grasses and pretty purple flowers that are in fact weeds.

Her stomach lurches as she drives past her husband and turns out of the driveway. She waves at Philip, smiles big like she is happy.

She had been. When she and Josh were dating, everyone said it was a match made in heaven. Her father, long widowed, his abuse fading away with his grief, now took Josh into his confidence. Threw a fat arm over his shoulder, told him he was getting the deal of a lifetime in his daughter. No one mentioned how dangerous a match might be in the wrong hands. It wasn't until years after they got married that the match ignited. A little, at first, small flames snapping. A child would help, Katie thought and then said. But she couldn't get pregnant. At first months, then years, and now here she is at thirty-nine, no kids, aflame.

Josh had made love to her on those days marked on the calendar with a heart. If she said she was feeling a little sick, he brought her cold water in bed. They didn't have money for fertility treatments or special doctors. They talked about selling land; their house was situated on the front end of a large double lot. It seemed like a hassle. Anyway, Josh had said, he liked having that space.

It's been three years since the last glass of cold water and they rarely use their backyard.

The market is a success. Katie sells almost everything. She'll continue taking a stall at the market, way better than an online store. She talks to so many people and they are all happy to see her. Later, as she putters back into the driveway, she notices that Josh's car is gone. Right, Andy's party. Should she go? Andy was Josh's friend, really, an old college roommate. She would unpack and then decide. Slipping her feet out of her shoes in the mudroom, she is elated at the house's emptiness. Once inside, though, her foot immediately stings. She feels the splinter in the soft of her foot before she sees the mess.

The hallway is covered with piles and piles of wood. Fragments, two-by-fours, dowels, slabs, her tools scattered like buckshot on the floor. She breathes heavily, sidesteps the collection, and begins to return the pieces to her workshop. No, she will not go to Andy's party.

After she is done getting her shop in order, she sits. The task has winded her. She checks her email and flips through social media on her phone. Ice cream cones in front of colored walls, carefully placed bikini bodies, latte art, yoga positions in faraway places, smiling children at dance recitals and on beaches. Then she sees a photo of Josh on Andy's feed. He is assisting a young blond with a frothy white drink. One hand is at the back of her neck, as if he's holding her up. Katie doesn't know who she is. She stands up, sits back down again, dizzy. She allows it to pass and slowly makes her way through the hall, now only the smallest shards of wood threatening each step, unseen. She tiptoes through the minefield, slips her shoes back on, and goes outside to her car.

When she gets to Andy's house, she can hear music even though her windows are rolled up. She goes around the side of the house and Marie is immediately at her side with a beer.

"So glad you could make it!" she exclaims. Katie shakes her head at the drink.

"Really?" says Marie.

"I think I'll just have a pop," Katie says.

"Pop. Ha. So cute. Your little Midwestern ways," Marie says and bounds onto the deck and returns with a sweating can of artisanal cola. Katie would've preferred a Coke. She scans the crowd. Several young blond women. A piñata shaped like a poop emoji. TLC's *Waterfalls* is playing. It had been a favorite when Katie was in school. She knows all the words and can't help but mouth them as she walks over the perfect grass, sidestepping lawn chairs, beer cans, and discarded tiny cocktail umbrellas. Men are playing beer pong with red cups. Who knew forty was so . . . Katie doesn't know how to finish this thought. She sees Josh alone in the shade of a tremendous maple tree, picking grass. She must have misunderstood the photograph. She approaches, smiling.

"Made it." She sits beside him. It takes him a moment.

"Hey!" he says and stares into the distance.

"I made, like, seven hundred bucks."

"That's great," he says, distracted. She follows his gaze. The blond from the photograph is headed straight for them, two drinks in hand. In her peripheral vision, Katie sees Josh shake his head at the woman, but she looks puzzled and continues toward them.

Crocheted bikini top, denim cut-offs, barefooted. Twenty-five, Katie would guess. Presumably one of the models that Andy works with. Her name would be Madison or Hayley. Maybe Taylor.

"Hi, I'm Hayley," she says and offers Katie the drink. Hayley isn't as dumb as she appears.

"Friend of yours, Josh?" Katie says and takes the drink from the girl, pulls out the cocktail umbrella, and puts the drink down in the grass behind her. She sucks the froth off of the umbrella. Piña colada. Katie twirls it in her hand, feels its sharp tip.

"Um, yeah, we just met. She's a nanny," Josh says.

"Is she?"

"I just love kids," Hayley says.

Katie is overwhelmed with nausea. Her every pore fills with sweat. Bile collects in her throat, like so much she wants to say, and she is unable to hold it in. She vomits. Hayley startles and jumps back. Says she'll go get some napkins.

She doesn't return.

Katie and Josh go home that night in one car. "We'll get mine tomorrow," he says. Katie sticks the cocktail umbrella in the radiator vent.

Perhaps she is pregnant.

At the doctor's office, she pees in a cup and they wave a wand.

"There's a small house in there," Dr. McManus says, as though announcing Katie needs to rotate her tires or change her oil.

"A house?" Josh asks, a puzzle on his face. He has come to the appointment. Katie thinks maybe they'd been right. Maybe a child will help.

"What are you talking about?" Katie says. "Am I having a baby, or what?"

"It is strange. I suppose you could call it a baby. You know, in this field, we see all kinds of things," Dr. McManus says, and leaves the room in a whoosh of sterile paper.

They sign a lot of paperwork. There are needles inserted into her abdomen, which, given the spate of recent splinters, is no big deal for Katie. Calendars are looked at, appointments made. She is a geriatric pregnancy, they tell her. She bristles at this, wants to punch them, but they say it with a smile, purple mouthed, saccharine—not real sweetness, but it tastes similar enough.

Katie pulls the little cocktail umbrella from the car vent. What a useless piece of shit. In bed she tears the canopy off the umbrella, snaps the little ribs that hold it up, purple bits of paper scattering around her on the bed like confetti. She unwinds a tiny piece of paper that looks like a very small Chinese newspaper. What she is left with is a toothpick. A sharp, thin piece of wood. She jabs herself; it draws a pinprick of blood to the surface. She puts the toothpick in her bedside drawer.

That night, in bed, Josh says, "Remember that time in Florida?" For their honeymoon, they'd stayed at a $700-a-night beach resort. Breakfast in bed, the sun baking them as they ate overpriced hummus platters by the pool. Cucumber never tasted so good. Two days in, she had stepped on a Portuguese man-o'-war and howled like a wolf. Josh carried her, always carrying her, across the dense sand, up the wooden stairs, past the pool and bar where they'd spent hours drinking frozen daiquiris, and into the cool marble-floored lobby. *Someone help us!* he had shouted. The concierge wore a suit, but he bent to her wet sandy body, made the right phone calls quickly, and it wasn't long before Katie and Josh were back at the poolside bar drinking daiquiris, hers now virgin because of the medicine she'd been prescribed. They laughed about it later, often, but Katie still remembered how much that sting hurt. Never before had she experienced such pain. Labor is worse, a friend had told her. Much worse.

I will protect you, was what Josh had said then and repeats in bed as he cleans the purple umbrella confetti from the sheets. From what, is a question Katie only now thinks to ask.

He does not apologize for the woodshop incident and she doesn't bring it up, but she still sees splinters around the floorboard edges, waiting to stab someone. At night, she pulls out the former cocktail umbrella and lightly pushes it against Josh's sleeping skin. He snorts and rolls over. She pushes again at the flesh on his upper arm; the skin starts to give, a tiny cleaving. He waves his arm in his sleep, mumbles, "Not today. I'm not ready." Katie puts the fine piece of wood back in her drawer.

At another barbeque, this time celebrating Andy's job promotion, Marie approaches Katie. "Wow, you're a house," she says, maneuvering her hands around Katie's girth.

"What?"

"You're as big as a house," she repeats.

There is no question; it will have to be a C-section.

They put it on the calendar on an otherwise unadorned Monday. There would be a full moon, the calendar told them. They look at pregnancy books, but when it says their baby should be the size of a lentil, a peach, a papaya, Katie thinks, this is not my baby. My baby does not look like a piece of fruit.

The full-mooned Monday arrives. Needles are installed in her body, drugs pushed in. In a surgery that lasts three times as long as it should, the surgeons pull a small wooden house out of Katie—a shack, it could be called.

At home, Katie caresses the shack and places it on the mantel.

"Are you sure that's the right place for it?" Josh asks.

"Don't you think I know how to take care of it? I carried it for nine months," she says.

"Ten," he says, and she staggers from the room, the staples in her abdomen itchy with fire.

The shack develops into a cabin which becomes a cottage and is showing all signs of healthy growth. Katie outfits it with small furniture, procured from online thrift shops and local estate sales. She makes the tables and shelves herself. She creates its own accounts on social media, @LittleHouseOnTheCherry. They live on Cherry Lane, and she finds her nostalgic wordplay hopeful. Her little abode has over nine thousand followers already. She sews tiny bedding and rugs. It is a lovely little place. Someone could fall in love with it, in it.

Josh grumbles about how much time she spends with the small house.

"This is what it needs," she says. "It needs its mother." He occasionally reassembles rooms and pokes at things that could become problems.

"I know houses," he says. She thinks, he does not.

Katie worries about its future. Would it become a McMansion? The same as everyone else on the block? Dance recitals, cute utterances, videos posted to social media? She approaches Josh with research.

"We could use the lot out back," she says. "It's getting bigger and we don't need the space and isn't that what we said we wanted it for when we bought the place?"

"I don't remember that," he says.

"We said that one day, we'd have children running around out back, naked in the sunshine," Katie says.

"But we don't."

"We do. Kind of," she says.

"I want my land," Josh says, and Katie clams up and stews quietly about what to do about her progeny.

It's growing colder; fall is approaching, and Katie sets a fire in the fireplace. Above, on the mantel, the little house is lit by tiny fairy lights. It is outgrowing the mantel, so she moves it to a nearby table. It looks homey and she thinks that so far, she is doing a good job of being a mother.

It is eight thirty and still Josh isn't home from work. Katie eats pickles from the jar and pushes to find any soft spots in the wood of her little house. She finds that it is pretty sturdy, no splinters jutting out from its baseboards or walls. She is proud of herself.

Then Josh gets home. She hears it first; he has hit the mailbox. He comes in staggering drunk, babbling and spitting about his unhappiness, leaning into Katie. If he stands close enough to the fire, he will ignite. A conflagration of their marriage, all at once. He points at the cottage.

He says, "This is just trash. It should be thrown out." He lunges for it. Katie is too slow. He shakes it and shakes it, pieces of furniture falling from its open windows. The door hangs by a screw and he rips it off.

"Josh! Stop!"

"It's not real, Katie." He throws the door into the fire.

"Stop! You're killing it!"

"This is not your baby."

"It is."

"It is not our baby," he says. She cries out, tears filling in every crevice on her face. Now that she is forty, there are more. Each split in her skin holding more, a deepening chasm. The aging body is a kind of topography.

Josh is shaking the house, profanities issuing from his mouth. He smells astringent, like a bathtub of gin. He pries off a piece of the roof, throws that in the fire, too.

"Stop it! Stop it! Stop it!"

"This is shoddy," Josh says. "Shoddy design, made like shit."

Katie has abandoned Katie's Kwality Wood. She only cares for the little wooden cottage now; she believes she is putting her best work into it. She spends late nights sketching designs, talking to it, though it does not talk back. Josh complains from their bedroom, stomping out to work in the morning without looking back.

The doorbell rings. Framed in the open doorway is Philip, the elderly neighbor. Katie and Josh stop, Josh holding the tiny house above his head.

"The door was open," Philip says, surveying the room. "The car door is still open, too." The crackling of the fire and the tick tick tick of the grandfather clock are the only sounds in the room, though Katie's heart is booming. Outside, a car whooshes by. Katie looks out the window, sees that the car door is indeed open, the interior dome light still on.

Josh lowers the house an inch and she snatches it. He storms out past Philip to the car. Slams the door shut, but stays outside.

"Thanks, Philip," Katie whispers.

"You're welcome, dear," he says and limps out, not even turning to look at Josh in the yard.

The next day, while Josh is at work, Katie pours a small foundation out back. Places the cottage just so. When he returns home, Josh doesn't say a word. A week later, she has people in to hook it up to water, gas, and electricity.

The house is still small. Katie returns to her shop to create wooden people. She sets them up in the house in tableaus of domesticity. Four of them at dinner together. One sleeping while the rest cook a surprise cake in the kitchen. The mother caring for a small wooden baby in a tub while the father gets the other wooden child ready for bed.

Every day a new scene. Josh comes and goes, occasionally commenting on how she is wasting her time.

Eventually someone knocks on their door. Katie rises to answer and is met with the fat pink face of a city official.

"I hear you have an illegal ADU," he says.

"What's an ADU?"

"Accessory dwelling unit."

She closes the door on him. But not two minutes later, she sees him in her backyard.

"You can't be here," she says. "This is private property."

"Ma'am, I have to issue you a citation."

"Fuck you," she says. "Get out of here." She slams the door, closes the blinds but watches through a crack as he measures her small house and takes notes.

"What do we got here," Josh says that night, as he comes in with a handful of papers. "This was at the front door."

"It's nothing," Katie says.

"Doesn't look like nothing," he says.

"Fuck it. Ignore it."

"I'm not going to ignore it. I don't want to be doing anything illegal, Katherine." There is grease in his mouth and his eyes have gone predatory. She recognizes the look immediately and knows she is the prey.

"You called," she says. "It was you."

"You yourself once said we could use that land to make money."

"You're an asshole." She gets up and pummels his chest. He doesn't strike back. Holds his hands up as if he is saying, I didn't touch her. I didn't do a thing. "FuckyouFuckyouFuckyou," she says. One jab knocks his glasses from his face. Another brings blood to his nostrils.

Three days later, Josh files for divorce. Katie tells him she won't sign anything. He doesn't come home from work the next day. Again she sees Josh on Andy's social media feed. He is prone on a deck lounge chair. Hayley is beside him. They aren't touching, but the smile on Hayley's face mirrors Josh's.

Katie calls Marie, who does not call her back.

That night, Katie hears voices from out back. Her little house has grown into a three-bedroom, two-bath, with a deck out back and an eat-in kitchen. As Katie steps into her garden shoes, she sees lights burning in the den, which she has outfitted much like her own: fireplace, L-shaped couch, coffee table with magazines fanned out. She looks back at her and Josh's house. All the lights are extinguished except in the kitchen. When Josh came in, she had been preparing herself a microwaved bowl of mac and cheese, a childhood favorite now rendered into congealed cheese sauce and undercooked noodles. The house out back looks warm and inviting. A light shines over the front door. Katie doesn't knock and turns the doorknob. The door gives and she follows the voices into the den. There is a man on the sofa with a book in his hand, thumb in the spot where he had paused his reading. He is assisting a woman, who is nursing a baby. The baby falls off the nipple and issues a bleat, which turns into a full-blown cry. The woman pats the baby's back, shushes softly into her ear. The man rubs her shoulder with his thumb. Katie sits on the rug in front of the fire, curls into a nautilus. She closes her eyes as the fire heats her skin.

The cries of the baby, her baby; she'd know that sound anywhere.

Postcards from the Person You Ate

At first, Margaret went around whispering about the rape. The rape? Her rape? Did she own it? Did she have to keep it? Did she share it? Could she leave it on the side of the road? Put it in the recycling bin? Margaret quietly spoke of the night when Marcus announced that her cunt was nothing but an open bar. Free for the taking. No payment necessary. Lush as all fuck, he'd said.

After that, Margaret would see Marcus around campus, arms slung around his bros and girlfriends. Great white horse teeth that people admired. The teeth that had chewed her, masticated her into a slippery wet paste, and spat her out.

In class, Margaret got dirty looks from self-righteous students as she mumbled while professors lectured about Hemingway or Ohm's Law. It was Marcus's posture that Margaret first noticed back in September. Now, a month after the rape, he sat in Econ with Laura Dykstra, their bodies slunk together shoulder to shoulder. Margaret whispered that Marcus was a vile animal. But no one listened; they only moved a few seats farther away.

Margaret stopped going to Econ. Failed the class, along with most others. Didn't tell her parents.

Summer break arrived. Margaret—now Maggie—decided to see America. To travel in her ten-year-old Jetta across interstates, stopping into houses turned into museums. Here is a photo of the old radium factory. Here is the very first saddle shoe. Here is a bronze bust of Mayor Bladwell. Here is the sash from the time a Winston resident won Miss America. Biggest Golf Ball in the World. Or at least in the country. Or the state, anyway. This was Lady Rhetta's sitting room. She took guests here. Maggie wondered what "took guests" meant. She asked. The gray-haired, self-named doyenne of Sampson Lake opened her mouth in a perfect fuchsia O and squeezed her eyes closed. No, miss, we're not like that here in Sampson Lake.

In Dubuque, in a frigid and stale motel room, under a sun-bleached print of a striped umbrella on a beach, as she flipped through Gideon's Bible, Maggie said to Gideon: "I am lonely." And in this loneliness, Maggie knew no one was listening to her, so she stopped talking—about her rape, and about anything else, too.

Instead of speaking, Maggie began collecting postcards.

"You gonna mail these?" a nosy motel housekeeper asked as she vacuumed the paisley carpet.

"Wasn't planning to," Maggie said, as she sat cross-legged on the bed.

"Don't go waiting for them to become valuable or nothing like that," the housekeeper said.

"What does it matter?" Maggie asked.

"Why keep track of where you been if you ain't lookin' to tell anyone?"

So, when Maggie's stack was significant, she decided to start sending them. *Wish you were here! Grand Canyon is . . .* she ignored the prompt and wrote what had happened to her that night, what Marcus had said when he proffered another drink and pulled at her underwear. She searched the internet for Marcus's address. She wanted his home address—his parents' house. Of course, a message sent by postcard would be picked up by the perfectly lacquered fingernails of Marcus's mother, and read.

Everything can be found on the internet, and Maggie found Marcus's suburban New York address, no problem. She wrote it in careful print on the postcard, wanting to be sure it got where it needed to go. Scottsdale. Taos. Park City. Twenty-five cents, thirty-five cents, a dollar. She bought glossy postcards, ones with canyons and sunsets and puns. Address. Stamp. Sign. Send.

Eventually, Maggie ended up in Skokie, where her mother said, "You've lost weight! You look great!" Maggie smiled without showing her teeth, which she now kept tucked away in case she needed to bite.

"You've got mail," her mother said, and led her to a pile on the shiny dining table. Thirteen of Maggie's faces looked down from the mantel. Kindergarten to graduation. Aside from sophomore year (braces), she could see her teeth in all of them. The mail in the pile mostly consisted of white legal-size envelopes. The writing was sloppy, but it had still gotten to her. She opened one. Read it. It said *What the fuck?* She opened the rest and there were many more *What the fucks?* and eventually some threat about legal action. Do it, Maggie thought.

But then realized she would have to talk louder if they did.

Her mother came back carrying a glass of water with a lemon peel curved over the edge. "Who are all those letters from?" she asked. Maggie took the water, chewed on the rind—tart on her tongue.

She didn't answer her mother's question, but Maggie began composing her story in her mind then, with the thought to share it soon enough.

Losing the House in D Minor

By the time my mother came back into the picture, we had already drowned.

First came the rains. Then, the deluge. Then, the constant wet. After we mired ourselves in the cleanup and after the insurance company bailed and after we tired of it in our bones, things only got worse. The whole town was dealing with it. My father's office dislodged from the earth and took off down a creek. Corporate decided not to open the branch again.

We couldn't afford to stay elsewhere. No one would want us, I was sure. First, the electricity fizzled out and never came back on. The water never warmed; it all slowed to a trickle and then stopped altogether. What was left were rusty trails where there used to be water, and those trails led to the pipes that mazed through the walls, and still, somehow, managed to drip inside the walls despite the faucets having run nearly dry. I'd hear it at night when I tried to sleep. *Dripdripdrip* and then *pingping-ping* as the droplets fell on some unseen metal. Ghost water, perhaps. Later, the floor in the half-bathroom buckled. Snapped.

Bayonet-like pieces of wood jutted up from the floor and dared people to enter. We told them not to bother because the toilet wouldn't flush. Visitors stopped coming.

My father was a classical music aficionado. When I was younger, he tried so many times to get me to appreciate it. *Listen. Listen here, do you hear the counterpoint?* No, no I didn't. I hated it, groaned theatrically when he insisted on impromptu lessons. But at this point, on a battery-operated radio, Bach's fugues were one of the only things alive in the house, not including mold spores.

Like abandoned asylums and neglected children's hospitals, our toys and heirlooms mingled with the weeds of neglect. They're flowers, too, those weeds—a kind of beautiful. *Glass half empty, half full*, my father would have said years ago, but now he says little and we don't have a clean glass, never mind water to fill it. The house was three thousand square feet. Two-car garage. Granite kitchen counters.

People started knocking at the door at all hours. Tonight they came at seven o'clock and my father shouted, *Don't you know not to come at dinnertime?* But we weren't eating and it reminded me that I was hungry. In the pantry, I found a can of white beans. I plucked them out of the viscous liquid and ate them, one by one. They looked like oversized maggots and I felt like I was eating from the carcass of our life.

The people at the door left, but I knew it was only a matter of time before they'd return. Perhaps with more people. Perhaps to take me away—I was only sixteen. Perhaps to take my father away—to lock him up, as if it'd be all that different from this jail in this subdivision where we seemed to be the only ones who couldn't salvage our old lives.

"What are we going to do?" I asked my father. Offered him some beans, but he just ate from a bag of barbecue-flavored chips. Sometimes he sucked on old hard candies, the kind that looked like little discs of gold.

"Wait," he said.

"Wait?"

"Wait. Not much we can do. Waiting. Dying. We're all dying anyway. From the minute we're born," he said. He occasionally did this, break into vaguely philosophical platitudes. But I knew he wasn't theorizing just then. He was actually dying.

"Dad, we can call Grandpa," I said. "He'd help." This wasn't true, most likely. My grandfather blamed him for the failed marriage and the subsequent departure of my mother. He never said so outright, but I know he had contact with her occasionally. Last time I was at my grandfather's apartment, I saw a photograph on the fridge of a woman smiling at the beach, holding a blue drink in a bowl. He caught me looking, but didn't say anything.

"Garbage," my father said. "He's a leech."

"But—"

"Absolutely not," he said, as he unwrapped a candy. He crunched his barbecue chips, wiped his hand on his shirt, and left what looked like claw marks against his chest. He switched CDs in the stereo and the room filled with the dismal tones of my father's preferred language.

I went in search of more food in the pantry, which was the size of a small bedroom but only contained a paltry supply of canned food, paper plates and napkins, a few jars of rancid spices. Still taped on the wall were faded, mildewed pieces of art from my childhood. Scribbles and dots deemed worthy of a gallery. My mom had put them up. They were over twelve years old; she left when I was four. Anyway, they were ruined now. I was searching for something to quell my hunger, but found little.

With each step through the house came an echo from when we were happy. When the framed photos on the wall weren't shrouded in a sticky dirt-like substance or fogged up. When the wallpaper didn't peel like an orange which, suddenly, you noticed was rotten on the inside. The peel didn't give that away— what was inside. It wasn't soft in your hand when you held it.

The cars were taken away on two different tow trucks. The SUV and the minivan. They had to manually open the garage with a crowbar and carjacks. We didn't go back into that space afterward. But I often heard scrambling, like mice or bats, and imagined the crawling habitat it had become.

I went out to collect the mail. The neighbor waved and I waved back but they didn't smile, so I didn't either. In the mail, circulars announced sales at the grocery store. White envelopes were punctuated with red and yellow and pink. They reserved these for people like me. My family, anyway. My father, really. It's just us left now in the hull of the house.

He got sick. I got sick. *Mold*, they said. But we couldn't do anything about it; we no longer had insurance. I traced my finger in the charcoal fungus that carried up the wall. In cursive, I wrote the name of my mother, as if calling to her. *Come back*, my message said.

I got better, marginally. Still needed my inhaler, but I left the house for much of the day. My father, he refused to use the inhaler, didn't want to—couldn't afford to—spend the money on the medicine, and sat wheezing in the creaking rocking chair, moldering blush-colored carpet beneath his cracked toes.

I occasionally visited my grandfather on the other side of town, but we never talked much beyond what I was studying in school and what sport was in season and how the local team was doing. I think he knew; I showered there, pouring creamy coconut shampoo on my head until the bottle emptied. Stuffed myself with whatever food he had: white bread torn and chunky with cold butter, syrupy peaches, and fruity low-fat yogurts from his fridge. I went to school. Did well—made honor roll (my father said exposure to classical music in children increases aptitude)—so no one noticed or cared. Came home from school and still the *scritchscratch* of the splintered rocking chair and the whistle of my father's sandpaper lungs came at regular intervals, just as it had when I left in the morning. The woodpeckers outside pecked staccato bursts against the house. I used the showers at school sometimes, too—after the doors were unlocked, before the other students arrived. Tried to fill up on free lunch, but they monitored that like we were in prison. Sometimes an extra packet of soup crackers wound up in my pocket. A few times, I plucked other students' half-eaten bags of chips from the trash. Filched rice crispy treats from the bake sale table.

I placed the mail on the dining table, on top of the already large and haphazard pile. Bills unpaid. Sales long past. Credit card solicitations. If there was a personal letter in the stack, we never found it.

"My batteries died," my father said by way of greeting. He caressed a CD as if it were a gemstone. Rainbows reflected on the ceiling; the house was otherwise surprisingly silent. And then, he coughed—a racking, doubled-over kind of attack. These attacks were becoming more frequent. The word *rattle* came to mind right away. Baby rattle, rattlesnake, death rattle.

Two days later, my grandfather came to the house. He let himself in, using a key given to him long ago. He didn't live far away, and I knew he had to pass the house to get from his apartment to the grocery store.

"Hello?" he called. I was sitting on the stairs reading "The Fall of the House of Usher," which seemed so perfectly appropriate. I devoured every word to find out what might happen to us. Because the staircase wasn't carpeted, it was one of the few places I could sit without the wet house seeping into my bones.

"What are you doing here?" I asked. Since the flood, though I visited him several times, he came to the house once and that was only to ask my father for money. He hadn't known the money would run out so soon. He was sent away empty-handed with the door literally hitting him on the way out.

But now, he was back. I wasn't surprised. I knew it was only a matter of time before he got involved. But I wasn't sure what his angle would be. He looked older than he was; skinny people do that, I've noticed. His hair was shock-white, long—to his chin— and thin; I could see his dark scalp underneath the strands. He usually wore a baseball cap, and I saw he had taken it off and held it in his hands, some old and weird ritual of manners. And then I saw he wasn't alone. The woman from the photograph with the big tropical drink stood behind him. My mother, who I hadn't seen in years. My mother. My mom. I did and did not recognize her. She was thin, wore only eye makeup, and her hair fell in a long straight sheet. I noticed I was taller.

"Louis, what is the meaning of this?" she said, bypassing me in the dark hallway. I was just a shadow on the rotting walls. She went into the adjoining living room, my father's space.

"My baby is sick. My baby is living like *this*? What are you doing to my baby!" she roared at my father as he rocked, rocked, rocked, and crunched, crunched, crunched. I wasn't sure who she was talking about. I checked her belly and saw nothing swollen. Was it me? Was I the baby? But no, here I am, Mom.

Here I am. I'm almost a man, I'm grown. I'm fine. See me. Touch me. Know me.

I'd been haunted by her for so long. Now, here she was, and she wasn't a ghost at all. She was a live person. My grandfather hung back, adjusting tilted pictures on the wall to make the house more presentable. I was old enough to understand that it wasn't me that my mother cared about. It was baby-me that she was worried about; the me she'd carried for ten months, the me she'd held on to when I cried as a toddler. It was the ghost of me. The real me, the living-and-breathing me, she wanted nothing to do with.

"Georgia," my father said. "Hi." He said this casually, and I admired him for it. He did not stand or make excuses.

"Georgia, I need some batteries. C," my father said. "Or D, maybe."

"Which is it?" she said. "C or D, Louis?" The curl of her lips looked like a smile, but I knew it wasn't.

"Let me check." He flipped the small stereo upside down. His earnestness was what she'd once fallen in love with. My father told me that on one particularly talkative occasion before the flood.

"Louis. What is this?" my mother asked. She didn't wait for an answer. "This is not okay. This house is not okay." He rocked and coughed and rocked some more.

"Georgia," he said, after a time. "I know this isn't what you wanted for *our* son." She tapped her fingernails against each other. They were shiny, pink—hopeful, as if she were about to go on another tropical vacation. I thought about the photograph on my grandfather's fridge.

I looked over at my father, saw him the way my mother did. In the shadowy afternoon sun, I realized his depression was greater than the weight of water and that he'd been sinking under it since long before the storm. After the storm, the depression sunk him completely, as if he had iron shackles on his feet. I thought I knew what it felt like: to walk across the ocean floor to see the life there, feel the muck between your toes. But I had no idea.

"You should go live with your grandfather," my mother said, finally turning her attention to me. My grandfather, too, had made his way into the room. She wasn't asking me a question, but I knew it was one. If I left, I would probably have to go to a different school. If I left, would I visit my father? The distance wasn't far, but once I was gone, would I come back?

I listened to the clock ticking, one of the few items that still functioned in the house, though its arms held the wrong time. My father wasn't looking at me. His breathing was accusation enough, wheezing, begging me to either cut off the pipe or clear the muck away.

"Why not with you?" I asked my mother, whom I skirted by so I could stand next to my father. I put a protective hand on his shoulder. Beneath the flannel, I could feel the point where his clavicle protruded at his shoulder. We had to map most of the 206 bones in the human body a few months ago in biology. I aced the test, but then forgot most of what I'd memorized. But I remembered the clavicle. What a whole lot of bones we were made of. All working together to keep us upright, most of the time. I lifted my hand, didn't want to feel the sharpness underneath. I walked the border of the room, running my hand along the walls. The mold hadn't yet arrived in here. In here, the twilight sung its bird song. In here, I felt the damp on my face, but could pretend it wasn't me crying.

"Well, *Mom*, why couldn't I live with you?" I said.

She didn't answer. Didn't need to. She didn't care. I knew if I chose to stay in this house, sooner or later, there would be repercussions. I said, "Well, that's that then, huh?" and headed toward the front door, but my grandfather blocked the way. I knew the house, though, and its many ways out. I turned around and left through the kitchen instead.

Outside, the rain began falling almost immediately. In that moment, I thought I knew what drowning felt like. Where would I go? Would I send postcards that said *Wish you were here!* and would my father be there to receive them? I walked for hours in the rain, making concentric circles in the blocks that surrounded our house. The rain eventually let up. My grandfather's car disappeared from the driveway. I heard music seeping out of the broken living room window. My father had found batteries. The music was unfamiliar. I thought I'd go back in and ask him about it. From this short distance, across the street and down a little, the house looked okay, save the overgrown weeds. And even weeds are considered beautiful, sometimes.

This Heart Hole Punch

I'm not a thief. The music in the craft store is playing Lionel Richie—a song my father liked to sing to me while he made me dance with him (not on the ceiling). The floor is white laminate and impossibly shiny. I can see my black shirt and red pants reflected back at me, but my face, well, I am unrecognizable; it's just a blur.

I have no money and I need supplies.

There are aisles and aisles of craft materials here. You can create anything you want. Stacked near to the ceiling with markers of all thicknesses, rough wooden shapes to paint and *make your own!*, fake leaves and flowers, so many kinds of papers of all weights and designs—argyle and paisley and polka-dotted and ombré. Also, feathers of neon from no bird that lives; I hate those most. Cans of spray paint are under lock and key, and children in heavy winter coats follow mothers with squeaking wet sneakers tracking in the dirty slush from outside. Older ladies lumber down the aisles picking up every ball of yarn, assessing whether they should use worsted weight yarn or heavy worsted weight yarn for their grandson's new booties. I know this because I was just asked by one of them. Apparently, I look like I knit.

I am in front of a staggering array of hole punches, mostly branded by Martha Stewart. I doubt she tested them all, but I like the baby blue and silver packaging. I get great satisfaction out of punching perfect shapes into paper. Leaving a void in a shape that is more perfect than what was there before. I lost all of my own hole punches in the move. One box missing, and it's that one. Now, I barely have enough money for food and I'm staying on the couch of the second cousin of a friend from back home.

I check to see if I'm alone in the aisle. Right now there is still a person down at the other end, looking at paper. I can't be too careful.

My father despised this habit of mine. He complained about the small dots that embedded into the carpet. Called me his little weirdo and made me pick the pieces up with my fingers, refusing to let me use the vacuum. He stood behind me and watched as I bent.

I moved to Seattle three days ago and I don't know anyone. I moved because they said it rained a lot. I wanted to be somewhere that wept all the time. Mom: died in childbirth—mine. Dad: died the day before my college graduation. With an inheritance that was just enough to move me somewhere new and live for a few months without a job, I went west. Isn't that what you do? Isn't moving across longitudes and latitudes supposed to heal you?

I hated my father, it should be said, and the healing I sought was far more complex than mourning.

The woman at the end of the aisle moves on. I'm alone.

As I look at the pegboard wall, I think about which hole punch I can pull into my sleeve. I pick one up, simple and green-handled, streamlined. I test out the theft, pulling my fingers toward my wrist, allowing the handle of the hole punch to graze my sleeve. Slowly I push and the tool disappears little by little, like I am pushing in a needle.

"Can I help you?" asks a store employee. I don't see her coming. The name tag on the green vest reads "Andie" and "Yorba Linda, California" in italics beneath it. I sound it out silently in my mouth and I like the way it rolls on my tongue. I pull the hole punch from my sleeve and clutch it in my fist. I tell Andie I'm looking for a hole punch, hold the green-handled one up as evidence.

"Well, you're in the right place," she says. I'm looking for something to punch into my skin, I want to say, but don't. "What do you need it for?"

"I need it to be strong. To cut through something heavy," I say, not fully answering the question.

"Well, these bigger ones—" She picks up hole punches that would require your whole arm to break something, anything; the base of the tool is the size of my palm.

"These are more for borders," she says. The ones she points to cut out trim with jagged teeth or with winding ivy—very Christmasy. I can imagine how pretty the paper would look, but that's not what I'm after. Anyway, they don't create holes, just snips along the edges; that's not enough. That's nothing.

"Yeah, I need something more for the middle, you know?"

"Yeah. The thing is, some of these aren't made so well. Don't tell my boss I said so," Andie says. "Maybe they'd cut, like, two pieces of construction paper at a time."

"I need stronger," I say. They all cost at least eight dollars and that's two meals at Taco Time. "And I need less expensive."

"Don't we all," Andie says. I look at her. A smattering of pimples across her forehead belies youth, but she looks tired—the kind of exhaustion that comes from living in corners.

When I was in high school, I spent many middle-of-the-nights walking the track at the school across the street. They kept the gates unlocked and the bright lights on all night, though the sign said it closed at eleven. Quarter mile, half mile, one mile, four miles. On and on went the night. Whatever I could do to be out of the house when my father, too, was home. He often worked the graveyard shift at the 24-hour pharmacy. Those were the nights I stayed in bed. I, too, had the fighting-demons-all-night look Andie has, when I was young.

I pick up a hole punch in the shape of a fleur-de-lis. It's so intricate I imagine it might actually tear the paper when you pull the utensil away from the paper. You can't be too delicate or the whole thing would rip apart and who would love you then?

I started with a simple, black-handled hole punch. The original. Tiny circular hole. Meant to make holes to attach pages together, to stick in binders, to tie with ribbon or fasten with brads. The morning after the first time my father came into my bedroom, I found the hole punch on the floor of my second-grade classroom. I pushed it against my fingertip, unsure of its purpose. Mrs. Sterling found me, cross-legged, silent, hair matted and unclean, and kindly said, *Here, let me show you.*

It was miraculous—the voids created in the paper where it was full before—and eight-year-old me asked to keep it.

I still have that hole punch, but it has grown rusty and takes too much effort to punch through paper. I already hung it on my new bedroom wall, which is, and will probably stay, otherwise unadorned. I packed it separately from the others, carried it with me.

I could just stop now. Now that they're all gone. Start fresh. I'd thought about it the whole way to the store. But the thought of being so unmoored makes me queasy and I decide I need one. Just one.

In the craft store, I survey the vast selection. Daisy, rose, cloud, dragonfly, pineapple, footprint, rabbit, musical note. Would I know what I wanted when I saw it?

Teardrop. Maybe it's a raindrop.

"Backup at front registers," a voice orders over the PA system. Good, let her go. I can't very well get the deed done with her staring right into my soul like this.

"There are some in the bargain bin," Andie says, "up at the front," motioning toward the front of the massive store. "Like half off . . . I gotta go. You going to be okay?"

I stare. Confused and feeling weirdly abandoned, despite the relief. As if we had this whole meaningful encounter and now I'd be left alone in the aisle, which might as well be an island in the middle of a vast ocean.

Maybe I'll take up something else. On the other side of the aisle is a rainbow of string, the kind used to make friendship bracelets when we were kids. I don't think I could manage that kind of hand-eye coordination, and anyway, who would I make them for?

I take one last look at the myriad hole punches in all shades of sherbet. These aren't what I want. Need. I tell Andie I'll be fine and watch her hightail it down the aisle as the overhead voice calls yet again for help. I select a few colors of string anyway. The names of the colors are musical: azure, raspberry, marigold, tempest. I scrunch them in my hand, deposit them into my pocket as I walk away.

At the front, I locate the bargain bins. One is filled entirely with hole punches. Reindeer, Easter eggs, jack-o'-lanterns.

Seasonal. Unwanted, now. Only wanted when the time is right. Otherwise, forgotten. All 75 percent off.

I pull out a heart hole punch. Valentine's Day. But hearts are for always, right? I take that one. It's small and would come to two dollars. I could skip a taco, get two instead of three. The shape of the tool is like the old-school hole punches, the kind you use by clenching your hand. It's not unlike what I imagine squeezing an actual heart to pulse it back to life is like. But instead of a circle, this hole punch makes a simple, tiny heart. I'm no surgeon, but it feels like I'm saving a life.

Outside I start with my receipt; it's the only paper I have on me. I feel for the string in my pocket, and walk and punch. The new tool feels right in my hand and cuts easily. I leave a trail of small hearts on the wet pavement.

Projection

Jackie's vagina projects films. All you need is a white sheet or screen. She discovers this as a teen, and she and her two best—and only—friends set up on weekend nights and laugh to Groucho Marx or the Three Stooges because it is old-school: not because they find it funny, but because none of them are the same anymore and this amuses them.

Jackie isn't sure how her vagina chooses the films; it seems completely out of her hands. While lying back, she clenches her fists and stretches her fingertips in hopes of having some sway over her vagina, but her vagina has a mind of its own. It/her vagina has a mind of its/her own.

Jackie often falls asleep during the showings; it hurts her neck to crane it just so and indulge in the movies. Her friends laugh and laugh, and at first offer a pillow, but then just fall entranced into whatever they are watching.

In college, Jackie's vagina wins all the icebreaker games. Jackie uses its ability to get friends, which is not intentional, but Jackie does not mind. In college, she has many friends; in this way, it is unlike high school, and she revels in it. Smiling wide, saying *yes, she'd love to come to their party*, when most of the time she would rather order pizza in and watch *Fleabag*, a show her vagina cannot or will not project.

She is invited to all the frat houses. She doesn't even have to remove her shirt. There, they watch movies based on comics— superheroes and mutants. It is loud, all that bashing and smashing and explosions. Jackie is the coolest, they say. High-five her when they see her on campus.

They forever pester her legs wide for their entertainment.

One night, in the hallway of the dorm, under a broken light, the gray carpet rough under her feet, she is stopped. There is a band she likes playing at the Union that night. She'd told her friends she would see them there. But instead she watches shadows on the skin of her hands change as the figure in front of her looms, sways.

"We want to watch a movie." There is a paperback copy of *Twilight* against the wall. Someone has lost their entertainment. She will take it, she thinks. Maybe ditch the show at the Union.

"Not tonight," she says, noticing that it is not just one guy, but several, moving toward her in a procession through the narrow hallway. They all look the same. A repeating sequence.

"Don't be a party pooper."

"I'm sure one of you has a Netflix account," she says.

"It's not the same."

"Bullshit." She stares at the apple on the *Twilight* cover.

"Nah," they say. They grab her body, shove her into the elevator, carry her out the front door. Tell the dorm guard Jackie is wasted. They laugh and the guard laughs and it seems everyone is having a great time.

They tighten their grip as they relay Jackie down the street, passing her from one guy to another. They smell of musk and beer and sing "Call Me Maybe." She'd loved that song when she was in high school; it sounds all wrong out of these sour mouths. She wants to yell out, wants to say *help* and *stop* and all the things she has been told to say but how can she say these things if they don't speak the same language?

Instead she says, "Hey guys, so what are we gonna watch?" They loosen their sweaty-fingered vises but do not let go of her.

In the frat house, they tie Jackie down, and as she squirms, the film wobbles on the screen as if a sheet is being shaken out, perhaps by a woman who had done the washing and is now folding the clean and lilac-scented laundry.

The movie is a comedy. Here is the synopsis: a man bumbles through dating, at once romancing a woman and then talking to his buddies about how frigid she is in bed. In the end, he buys her flowers, she bats her very long eyelashes, and a montage of wedding photos ensues.

Jackie's head hurts and the boys are pounding red cups. Except they are not boys but men in boys' costume. She tries to parse French conjugations as they watch.

> *je suis*
> *tu es*
> *il/elle est*
> *nous sommes*
> *vous êtes*
> *ils/elles sont*

Jackie changes verbs.

> *je prends*
> *tu prends*
> *il/elle prend*
> *nous prenons*
> *vous prenez*
> *ils/elles prennent*

Everyone in the room erupts into seething laughter. She changes again.

> *je donne*
> *tu donnes*
> *il/elle donne*
> *nous donnons*
> *vous donnez*
> *ils/elles donnent*

She gives up and her heart sends herself up near the ceiling. She refuses to look down at her prone body. They used to smoke here, she thinks, a faded khaki ring on the wall eight feet up. A light fixture with four of its five bulbs burnt out. Cobwebs like ladies' hosiery draped on the crystal pendants, dull with dust. It must've been pretty once. She flicks a finger at one of the pendants, wanting to make music, but this floating version of herself is insubstantial, powerless.

The movie ends. In the middle of the credits, there is one more scene. Two toddlers, diaperless with marker Jackson Pollocked on their bodies, run around while the man drinks beer with his friends and they laugh and laugh and laugh. The woman is nowhere to be seen.

Jackie whispers, "Je vais."

The boys sit back and pop open another can of beer. The smell of yeast and sweat fills Jackie's nostrils. She clenches her eyes and her fists and her Kegels and the credits of the film sputter like an old-fashioned projector, used up, spent. The boys groan. Swear. Go, you are useless now, they say, squeezing the empty cans in their greasy fists.

Outside in the air, she hurries away from the frat house, a little sore, alone. The smell in the air is the wet soil smell of rain—petrichor. The smell of life and earthworms and tree bark. Three blocks away, the rain begins as a mist. Four blocks away it escalates to a fat cleansing deluge. Eight blocks away, she realizes she isn't walking toward her dorm. Ten blocks away she thinks to hell with her phone. Realizes the phone is back in her dorm room. Twelve blocks away she decides she's going to keep on walking, see where she ends up.

Winter Rebirth

The baby is born at home. This isn't planned. In a blizzard in Wisconsin, she slips out of her mother and is wrapped, a slush of vernix and blood, in a white towel. The mother's womb begins to pulse, trying to get back to its place in her empty belly. Before she learned of the news. Before the child took shelter in her womb. A squatter, the mother thought of the life inside her. Even with the child out, the pain lingers. She says, *Where is my husband? Whereismyhusband*, she breathes.

The next moment, the baby is held by another and then another. There are three others in the house: cat, sister, neighbor who is a nurse. The husband, the other other, is gone. Save for the small band of gold and chip of a diamond on the mother's finger.

The mother nurses the child with drips of colostrum, and it is enough. It will be enough, even though the baby arches her back and demands more. Even though the mother arches her back and demands more, too.

The mother is on the towels and sheets piled on the faux-wood floor. All of her is spread far past her normal constraints. The room smells of iron and sour milk. A contorted version of her face looks back from a mirror. Is it the mirror or her face that is wrong? The mother's DNA breathes beside her, outside her. The baby is making stuttering yowls; the mother thinks it is shouting *Is this it? Is this fucking it?*

Eight months ago, the husband went out for the mail, for groceries, for gas. Gone to the liquor store, to the hospital, to the cemetery in a box. Dirt poured. A flower tossed, petals already browning at the edges.

"I do not want it," she says of the baby girl. The sister and neighbor take the small body and wash it free of the wet debris of birth.

"I do not want it," she repeats. It cries again, perhaps calling to her dead father, who was not perfect but was all the mother had.

"I do not think I want her," the mother whispers.

The mother limp-crawls to the bathroom for relief, of her bowels, of her arms. Sees her husband's dandruff shampoo in the shower stall. Misses the tiny snowflakes on her black shirts.

She should check on the child every two hours, they say. Nurse the baby, take it to your breasts.

They—she and her husband *they*—had wanted children in that faraway place called One Day. One day, when he would cut back on his hours and on his drinking. One day, after they were done with midnight dancing to the radio, kneading misshapen bread loaves, and clinking champagne flutes because it was a Wednesday. One day, when she felt prepared and he could hold her for hours as she wailed the banshee cries of childbirth and motherhood.

After he died, the mother had not wanted the child. Not really, and it had been too late to do anything about it when she emerged from the tunnel of her grief.

The blizzard keeps her sister and neighbor in the house. Help is close, in the next room and the next room after that. The preponderance of rooms, absurd with such an abridged family: mother, child, cat.

The mother has barely closed her eyes—a blink, really—when she hears the baby cry. The mother lies still; her body is so tired. Her hollow abdomen cramps and even her toes feel a sudden emptiness. Might she close her eyes again? Return to the dream that had not yet begun? Yes, she would. The baby will stop crying. But the baby doesn't stop. Bleats like a baby goat. The neighbor comes in. Hair knotted, still wearing the clothes she arrived in—the stay wasn't planned. At the bassinet, she shushes and pats. The mother hears the thumps on the back of the baby that sound too hard. Aren't they too hard?

"Are you hurting her?" the mother asks. The neighbor brings the bundle to the mother, who rolls to her side and takes in the creature. It latches with ease. The neighbor waits on the edge of the bed. The mother and baby fall asleep. The mother wakes a few hours later; the friend is gone, the weight of the bed uneven again. The baby is in the bassinet. The clock reads two hours later than it did when last she looked. The mother rises while the baby sleeps. The child is fine. The mother watches it in the lines of light from outside. The mother lifts the blinds; it is still snowing.

The mother is hot, despite the tremendous winter outside. She presses her cheek to the windowpane, watches her breath as it clouds. Opens the window, snow has collected at an angle in the crook of the pane. With her fingers she digs into the snow. Wet and virgin. She takes a small snowball into her mouth. The baby, would it die if it fell into this snow? The drifts. The snow that keeps coming. Would the baby die? If so, would it be hypothermia or a broken neck or drowning?

The baby wakes. The mother leaves the window open, takes the child to her bed, to her breast. They fall asleep together again, but there is no one to remove the child.

In the morning, the mother wakes with her nipple out, small wet stains on the sheets, her breasts engorged and radiating. The baby next to her, her mouth still formed as it had when it was nursing. Pursed tiny lips. Curled fists. The mother wonders about smothering, in the sheets, under her body; the mother imagines the baby falling off the bed. And then it wakes. They begin again.

The snow has stopped. The neighbor trudges home. The sister, too, with promises to check back in. In the empty house with expansive rooms and the stain of birth in the living room by the ottoman—the mother will cover it with a rug but return to it frequently—the mother and the baby make their introductions. The snowplows scrape the street outside.

The mother's legs are still sticky, twelve hours later, with afterbirth. Her body aches and throbs everywhere. Even still, she keeps forgetting about the child. Then her breasts become thick and pulse with need. She takes her child to her. Feels the relief and the pain that comes with providing for a newborn. Looks at the bassinet, the perfect lacy bassinet—picked out by the husband the day before his last. At her breast, the baby falls asleep and the mother puts her not in the bassinet, but beside her, on the husband's side of the bed. The mother, in that moment, feels like a mother, but then she looks away and doesn't.

The Joke

How's the joke go? Doctor, it hurts when I do this. And the doctor says, then don't do that. Mark says the insomnia is in my head, and I wonder if that's worse. Hysterical, women are always so hysterical.

It's 3:14 A.M., and when I bang my head on the headboard, I feel something shake loose. Mark, long relegated to the guest room, snores and only occasionally asks in the morning why there is a blossom of a bruise on my forehead and why the long face? My right eyelid is permanently drooped, having been forced to see things it didn't want to.

I say tonight will be different. But it's not and *boom* goes a thunderclap. Where we live now, this doesn't happen often. Where I grew up, there were storms every night, but here it will make the news. As the storm rolls around our house, it tosses the shutters and downs power lines and trees. I close my eyes and my nervous system turns into a dahlia—all segmented pieces bursting from the center and hard as fuck to grow, but if you do, people will tell you all the time how beautiful they are.

My daughter sleeps in the next room where underwater sounds issue from a machine and at 3:16 A.M. I think, *please don't drown please don't drown please don't drown.*

I turn on the lamp, grateful the power hasn't gone out. I survey my toolkit: an award-winning novel bookmarked at page 17 like it's been for a month. The dried carcasses of old contact lenses, blue and useless. My grandmother's Bible, stripped of its cover and embraced in dust. I have nothing.

At 3:24 A.M., Mark stumbles into the room. This happens often. He sees the light as an invitation.

"You okay?"

"No."

"No?"

"I'm fine."

His eyes are hoods, only seeing a fraction of what I do. He sits on the side of the bed.

"You need help. I can offer some assistance." He has on his I-want-sex voice. He drags his fingers along my side, protected under the comforter we purchased together. I hate it. It's maroon and gold paisley. His choice, but he doesn't even sleep in here now.

"Mark, I'm not really in the mood."

"Oh, I don't mean—" he says. Yes, he does.

At 3:31 A.M., he is done, already rolled off me and snoring atop the comforter, leaving me underneath, pinned like a butterfly, arms above my head, legs wide.

I laugh—one might say, hysterically—but he doesn't wake. I flip through the flimsy pages of my grandmother's Bible for some insight, but all I get is an inhalation of mites. I stick a dried-out contact in my eye and let it burn. I do the other eye, too.

I make a doctor's appointment in the morning. My husband can't understand the pain of wakefulness. What's the joke's punchline? It hurts when I do this. No, that's not right; the punchline is: So, don't do that.

So, maybe next time I'll sleep through the night.

Here We Sell Hands

I was wrapping up a transaction; a woman was buying a pair of hands to braid her granddaughter's hair, when an old man shuffled in—suspenders, cane. I tied the woman's bag with twine, handed it over with a smile. *No returns. Have a nice day.*

"Can I help you?" I asked the man.

His limbs shook. He held tighter to his cane with both hands as his rheumy eyes swept over me and the shop. He cleared his throat the way that old cars do when they're starting up.

"Greatest selection of hands in Door County."

"Just looking," he said. Coming into a hand shop, unlike, say, a bookstore, requires intention. I thought he, like my previous customer, might want hands to do what he could no longer do, the tasks old age makes cruel: shaving, opening jars, using the toilet.

It wasn't long before he spoke. "Got this son-in-law," he said. "And, well, my poor Ilana . . ." He tapered off, coughing over the omission. We talk and talk and what's not said is the loudest. But watch the hands, they speak volumes.

I use my products, too. Sometimes I pretend I'm a lefty. I wanted to know what it was like to wear nail polish, so now I use my "Generic Female, Polish" when I feel the need. But while working, I use my own. Professional.

I got into this business when my wife left with Hannah. My own hands rubbed her back, brushed her hair. But Hannah knew they were just an imitation of the hands I wanted them to be. Haven't seen Hannah in years. I bet she swings from monkey bars and pops bubbles for fun.

The man was looking at the Shooting Hands.

"These are popular," I said. It was true that several criminal investigations wound up at my door. When I opened shop I was morally against the Shooting Hands. Now I realized I needed money more than I needed morality. If I was going to get my girl back, my business had to be successful.

People generally bought hands for two reasons: for a task someone could no longer do but once could, or for a task they felt badly about. Grief can be tactile, and people think if they use other hands to commit their sins, their guilt will be mitigated.

"I need strong hands," the man finally said, picking up the thick callused hands of a manual laborer.

I had in mind that he wanted to throttle his daughter's husband. That his son-in-law was an asshole, an abuser. Hands worked like that. Made the impossible possible.

He opened his wallet, not without difficulty.

"Want a hand?" I ask.

"Fuck you. I got it," he said, but he didn't. Not really, and while he was working the intricacies of the wallet, an accordion of baby photos spilled out.

"Just trying to help," I said.

"Stop," he said and then threw his wallet to the ground.

"Won't let me hold my own grandbaby. Barely lets me touch her." His watery eyes filled, but no tears fell. "I raised Ilana by myself." I bent to pick up his wallet. "You hear me?" he said.

"I understand," I said. I didn't. I hated that I didn't.

I placed his wallet in his chest pocket, led him to the caretaker section, and showed him several Soothing Hands options. I pointed to one pair in particular, explained its subtle difference.

"I can see what they do," he said. I said nothing in return. Cars and trucks whooshed past on the six-lane road outside, rattling the windows. A thud from the shop on the other side of the wall—a mini-mart specializing in beer and bait. Then I heard the staccato rat-a-tat of the man's cane on the floor.

I placed my hand on his, and he steadied himself. I expected him to shrug me off, but he didn't. I felt the soft give of his veins, his fading elasticity. I saw the places his hands had been, the scars that weren't visible.

I sold him new hands. Wrapped them carefully in delicate tissue, tied the bag with twine, handed them over. I looped the handles between his fingers and closed them around it. I did not mention our return policy. Head in my hands, I listened to his cane's leaving song and the jingle of the bell above the shop's door.

Alone again, I picked up a pair of Soothing Hands—the kind most people have but don't realize. I put them on, taking care to cover my own skin completely, and used them to dry my face.

A Man Who Helps the Neighbors

The crow tilts its head and looks at me with its onyx eye, saying, yeah, you saw it, too, I know. I know you want to say, oh
he was just helping with the plumbing under her kitchen sink,
just patching up her siding. Her siding is what got you into this
trouble in the first place. In the first place, it was Celeste and
she was the landlady and she was all, to tell you the truth, I am
just useless without a man. A man who, when you married him,
everyone said was worth his weight in gold or at least in Micro-
soft stock because it was 2009 and that was a thing that meant
you had great value and anyway, he didn't have a stock portfolio
and neither did you. Did you think it wouldn't matter because
you had love? Love, as you now know, is for chumps, and now
you think it might be time to go but you won't admit it to anyone
else because he's just cleaning her gutters—it's so hard for her
to reach those places. Those places where a woman can't reach
but, oh, sure, a man can, a man certainly can reach those spots
hardest to get to. Get to the point, he says when you're talking.
When you're talking he rolls his eyes like the most delicate of

teenagers. Teenagers like you used to be, years ago when you hung out by the community garden outside the high school with him. With him, you smoked cloves and nibbled on chard you both were too proud to call bitter, and, when the season was right, you ate not-yet-ready blackberries and talked about how obviously no one told the gardeners that blackberry is a weed and if allowed, will grow and grow and take over with its tart juicy berries and its sharp-as-fuck thorns that got caught in your hair and drew blood from your skin. Your skin. Your skin was so young, dewy, elastic, soft—the skin of a child. A child neither one of you wanted. Well, you wanted it, but you didn't say. Didn't say since you'd both decided no, no children. No children in this house. This house is mine, he said. He said, I paid for it and I don't want any kids mucking it up. This is what we wanted, right? Now, you realized you've changed your mind about the baby and you wouldn't, couldn't get over the miscarriage and he was like, you just fucking mope around the house and burn chocolate chip cookies like you're Betty-fucking-Crocker's fucked-up sister and that is why I went to Laura. Laura says its time for you to get over it. It's funny to hear advice on a dead baby from the woman fucking your husband. Your husband is surprised when you carry three suitcases and a duffel bag out to the car. The car is yours, you tell him. You tell him you're leaving him and also point out that Laura's house is brick and doesn't have siding and I don't know anymore who you are. You are not at all clear on who I am. I am not for you. You are, he said. He said he loved my thighs and my fiery road rage and the way I ate the frosting off cake first. First, there was love.

Love, you said.

You said, calm down.

Pieces of Her

Her long seaweed hair, now freed of her body, stuck to the white subway-tiled wall of the shower in fine brown swirls and curlicues. At the center of the elaborate design, the hair looped to form double Ls. A tangle beneath the word, an underline. An emphasis. Pink mildew colored the grout in places, and determined water droplets clung to the tiles as if for life, refusing to fall. There were other designs, too—abstract flowers made of her pulled locks, maybe roses, maybe hydrangeas in their angry beautiful balls.

Hello, her hair read.

That's what she wanted to tell me? Hello, I am here. I am still here. But you aren't, I wanted to say. But I also didn't want to lay blame.

Along the side of the tub were bottles of shampoos and potions, grapefruit and peppermint. A bar of soap with her fingerprints still pushed into the aloe and jojoba, imprinted whorls of her. Her razor, blade up.

It had only been a week. This was the first time since she died that I dared to take a shower. I didn't want to take away her words, but already the moisture was causing her hair to droop.

I pushed my fat finger against a swirl of it, pushing it upward. Sticking it to the tiles. *Stay.*

I'd always thought it gross to find mats of her hair—stringy, dangly pieces, strands of dead skin cells—covering the shower wall. *I don't want to clog up the drain,* she'd say. I bought a hair trap, but that didn't stop her.

Later, during treatments, I noticed that the fine bits of hair on the shower wall had become fuzzy spiders—an infestation of her.

When the air in the bathroom cooled, and as soon as the water evaporated, her hair began to slip down the wall. The double *L*s slithered downward. The *O* withered. Soon, it would just be *he.*

I rummaged through a junk drawer, pushed aside paperclips and souvenir magnets of places we never got to visit. In the back of the drawer, I found a roll of clear packing tape. I cut the tape and laid it over her word. Smoothed it out so that there were no wrinkles or air bubbles.

After a week, moisture got trapped under the tape. I could barely make out the hair. Her *hello* was only some darkness slopped onto the white tile, a blemish. It was not the beautiful thing that my wife was. Is. Was.

I stopped showering, willing the hair to dry out. I wanted to feel her there in the shower with me, her violin backside, soaping herself and then me. I wanted to pull her into me and play her music.

But then a corner of the tape came loose, flapped in the breeze made by the uneven windowsill. Every other second, it would crinkle. Slap the wall. Otherwise the house was quiet. I pushed it back down. Pressed another length of tape down over it. But the walls were too damp. The hair remained, trapped, creating its own ecosystem. It looked disgusting. I left it anyway.

A few days later, the tape came loose again, and when I saw it in the mirror—wilting plastic, scraps of hair stuck to it—I squeezed my fingers into my palm, leaving half-moons where the nails pushed in. I shoved the glass shower door aside, and it rolled on its track and slammed into the wall.

Goddamn! I grabbed the flap, pulled at it. *Fuck!* Ripped another piece down. *Why?* And another. The tape caught on my arm hair and I yanked it off. It smelled like rot and mildew and pineapples and I remembered when we went to Hawaii on our honeymoon and she ate pineapples until her lips puckered.

And then the whole mess came off the wall, tape and hair and damp. I fell, the floor wet beneath me. I breathed. The persistent drip from the shower head. *Drip. Drip. Drip.* Down into the hollow gullet of the drain. I carefully pulled each strand from the tape. It no longer said *hello.* Or even *he.* It was nothing but a balled-up, dead fragment of her.

Some of the hair had broken when I pulled it from the tape. I held it in my hand, these—I counted them—thirteen—fragments of her. Her hair had been auburn and thick. Brown indoors, but once the sun hit her head, it shone like a polished piece of mahogany.

Thirteen flimsy pieces. That was it. I held the pieces of her in my hand. They were so fine. Delicate. Easy to break. Nothing like her. I clenched my fist. Held her tight. Clutched her last remaining fibers. All of her could never really fit in the palm of my hand, I knew that. Our life, our marriage, our love, our sex, our laughter, our pain.

I moved aside the hair trap, fed each piece of hair down the drain, one by one. Until the only thing I had left of her was everything else.

The Sound of Nouns

The adjectives are the first to go. *Pretty. Lovely. Sad. Angry.* Then, the verbs. *Walk. Talk. Breathe.* Later, adverbs go, too. Eventually, your hearing is whittled down to strict nouns, not even pronouns. *He* and *she* and *I* dissipate into the noise of the world.

When you begin to lose your hearing, you think *this is not happening* and *could you please just speak louder.* You turn the volume on the television up. When you begin to lose your hearing, you blame headphones and loud concerts in your twenties. When you begin to lose your hearing, you are accused of being aloof, snobby. When you begin to lose your hearing, you feel like you're slowly going crazy. Alone.

With your wife, you visit the doctor. The doctor scribbles *presents with aphasia.* You ask what that is and all you hear is *stroke.* Your wife kneels at the doctor's feet, leaving you with your naked knobby knees hanging off the table. She is crying. You don't hear it.

You are a writer and your recent novel has been acclaimed by the critics, but you've received seventy-three emails from

73

people who are angry. Sheila, your protagonist, was initially a man's idea of female perfection. Indeed, that was your intent, but it seemed one-note. So, you changed course and made her the victim of despicable domestic abuse at the hands of her husband, leading to life in a motel which led to a gig as a stripper which led to prostitution. You felt you were being honest, empathetic. Sheila's ex-husband, an attorney, continued to go to ball games and islands and had great white teeth you could see at a distance. In the end, Sheila killed herself. You thought this was poetic.

Your daughter is a college sophomore, and you yearn to tell her about the one-in-five sexual assault statistics you've read about in your research. You are terrified for her. She writes you a letter, citing things she's learned in her Intro to Women's Studies class, and noting how you've perpetuated the weak female stereotype. *I fucking hate your book*, she types in bold italics, underlines. You try to talk to her, but you can't speak on the phone. You tried. You can only hear every third or fourth word and so the conversation is stilted. She is several states away. Your new loss is bigger than the distance.

The next week, you have IVs inserted, dyes pushed through your veins. You have a scan. First one, then another. They find nothing alarming. You only know this because they write it down in barely legible handwriting on personalized notepads. Your daughter flies in—taking two planes—from her small college town. She and your wife have covert conversations after dark in the kitchen. The doctors mention mental illness. A psychiatrist's name and number is handed to you. Your wife looks at you like you are a child faking sickness to get out of school. She goes back to work, from which she had taken a short leave of absence. Your daughter returns to school.

You begin your third novel in the basement with a drop ceiling and twitchy fluorescent lighting. You don't answer the phone or the door. You keep writing. It is true that with the selective hearing your writing has gotten more succinct. Less meandering, more effective. You write about a world filled solely with women. It's rather incredible and might be a place you'd like to visit, but you know you're not the expert. You add in a few men. They are rattling vessels made up of spare parts of yourself. You set the story aside with a click of the X and go upstairs to make dinner for your wife.

In the kitchen, you prepare a beef stew. The house smells like bay leaves. When she gets home, your wife says *vegetarian* and *years.* She doesn't eat the stew and instead cuts cubes of cheese; they are perfect one-inch squares. You let the succulent meat melt between your teeth. It will taste better tomorrow. She says *therapy.*

The psychiatrist's office is in a shopping mall with a one-way mirrored window looking out into the main corridor of the mall. It is such a strange diorama, to survey a mall, the most public of places, while you are meant to divulge your most private of secrets. It is disconcerting, but you are fascinated and take mental notes to use for your stories.

As you expected, the meeting is challenging. After the psychiatrist says *couch, seat, hearing,* you both come to the understanding that writing out the conversation is the best approach. Speech has also been difficult since your new deafness. You haven't written by hand in a while, and your fingers grow tired quickly. Next time, you tell yourself, you'll bring the laptop.

I know Dr. Moreland thinks your hearing loss may be psychosomatic, the therapist writes. He offers you the pen. It is like an accusation. The utensil is a Montblanc—thick, expensive. You don't take it. *What do you think*, he scratches. The letters are jagged and he leaves out the question mark, as if he doesn't expect you to answer. You wonder what this says about the doctor. He offers the pen again. You reach down to your bag and pull out your Bic with the chewed end.

I wouldn't invent this, you write.

You're a writer, I know. Could this be some kind of writer's block?
No.

Tell me about your childhood.
No.

What follows is a silence bloated with expectation. You get up from the couch and look out into the mall. Two boys, maybe eighteen, sit in giant leather massage chairs. One is on his cell phone. The other keeps swinging his head to follow nearly every woman as she passes by. A girl, about thirteen, walks by and the head-swiveler smacks the phone-user for his attention. Words are not necessary to see that they are sizing up this girl. Head-swiveler licks his lips. Your mouth goes dry.

Behind the boys is a clothing store. Two women, at least ten feet tall, peer out from the advertisement. *Jeggings!* it shouts, excited. A few artificial orange maple leaves are scattered in the window display. The women's backsides are shown, their faces are looking back at you over their shoulders in a coy, come-hither look. *Flattering favorites for every fall look!* they cry out.

Your daughter wears jeggings. You once scolded her for wearing them, saying you could see everything you shouldn't in such tight pants. They will only bring you negative attention, you told her. She asked you to be more specific. You let it drop.

Boyfriend. Class. Professor. Econ. This was the gist of your most recent conversation with your daughter. You said a stumbling goodbye and handed the phone back to your wife. You cried. Your daughter is the real reason you are in the psychiatrist's office down a narrow hallway in a shopping mall in suburbia.

The psychiatrist is nudging you with the pad of paper. You turn around, but don't take it. You read, *How do you feel about medication? I think I know something that may help.*

You shake your head, say out loud, *Thank you for the visit,* and leave his sanctum. Out through the waiting room, past the Matisse print you know is called *Blue Nude.* You feel your heels click on the shiny mall floors. You feel traction under your shoe. You have stepped in gum. There are other dark blotches on the floor you assume is gum of teenagers past. This affects you in a way you couldn't have predicted. In the buzzy silence of the mall, you crouch down and try to get nearer to the gum that has captured you. Not close enough. You sink to your knees and allow your chest to graze the floor. You hear the words *help* and *security* and look up. Two security guards are headed in your direction.

You get close to the wad of gum. You want to smell it. If you get close enough, can you smell the flavor? You scrape at it with your fingernail and it comes up easily; it is bright purple under the dirt black. Grape, like children's cough syrup. The security guards are reaching for your arms. They lift you. You can see they are asking if you need help, but you can't hear their words. They say something about your health and age as you feel the gum in your fingertips. Its tackiness is satisfying and you shirk off the guards' hold. You nod at them and carry on through the mall.

Your writing suffers. At first it's minor connection issues, nothing a little studied wordsmithing won't help. Then, it begins to announce itself, despite your best efforts to keep to the plan you had laid out. Your female characters are the first to exhibit symptoms. They begin saying things that you would've normally attributed to your men. *Delete. Delete. Delete,* you press, but when you retype, you only type the same words again. You close your laptop. You open it. The dialogue is still there. You close your laptop. You feel remnants of gum on your fingers. You realize that *suffer* is the wrong word. You open your laptop. You change your plot and characters altogether. You email your editor, who writes back immediately. He isn't pleased. You don't care.

You find your wife at the kitchen sink. Hug her from behind, hands encircling her waist. You rest your head between her shoulder blades. You say you're sorry.

Your hearing situation does not improve. You can't hear much of what's being said, but you make do. You cook lentils and beans for your wife. You email your daughter links to more statistics. She writes back: *I know, Dad* and tells you she is majoring in women's studies. She writes that she is minoring in creative writing. Your heart skips. You tell her the new plotline of your next book. She writes: *def improvement!* and does not use bold italics or underlining, but does use an exclamation point.

In your selective hearing, you realize, there is no ownership. There is no selfishness; no *I.* No judgment. The women are not fat, or skinny, or beautiful, or ugly. The men are not sexy, hairy, scary. Your entire plot has changed. And, you've decided that it's not a bad world to live in: a world where men and women don't always do what you expect them to.

The Ink That Doesn't Dry

The tattoo on her finger read: *Breathe*. I thought it was poignant. But I'd had enough margaritas to make me brave, and so a reminder to do something that was pretty much involuntary seemed like poetry.

The lights were dim and yoga-studio music floated through the air—flute and waterfalls, or rain, and I think a frog's croak every so often. I remember the music because I thought it'd be heavy metal or something. But the space I stood in was more like a spa than what I thought a tattoo parlor would be. Beyond the main room were smaller rooms they called studios. That's where the branding would happen.

I scribbled a sad excuse for a signature and handed over a credit card and my ID.

"You're from Jersey?" she asked. Well, yeah, my ID said Hoboken, didn't it?

I smiled and said, "Unfortunately." That was the right answer; she tapped her lip ring with a sharp nail and laughed. She took my hand and led me into a studio. I was surprised I wasn't given a plush robe and tea.

"Me, too. Bergen County. I'm Raine." Raine had both arms covered. Full sleeves, she called it. On her right arm, a copper-headed mermaid stared back at me. She smirked while I grimaced at the thought of the pain. She looked like an anime character.

"That's me when I was a child," Raine told me when she saw me studying her arm.

"She doesn't really look like you," I said. She didn't. Raine had blue-black hair and her eyes weren't nearly as cartoonish as the mermaid's.

"It was the me that never got to live," she responded. She brought me a binder. For ideas, she said. She didn't elaborate on her comment. I didn't ask her to.

I took the binder. Flowers and frogs and several sea-themed designs filled the pages. There weren't many sailors left in New York and still, Raine told me, they inked quite a few anchors. "Guess people really need anchoring in their lives."

Toward the end of the album, I found more intricate illustrations. Vibrant teals and crimson, details that I couldn't imagine being able to see, no less draw. Broken teeth within witchy faces. A small snail peeking out of some reeds. Entire poems. These were unique. Created especially for the customers, Raine said.

"Wow," I said, truly in awe. Growing up in a Jewish household, tattoos were "verboten." This was the word my father used. Not only did Jewish law forbid bodily desecration, but the memory of blue numbers haphazardly spread across worn forearms made a Jewish kid think twice, three times, a million times, before considering a tattoo. I had always thought it was something I would never do. My father's parents were in the Holocaust. His mother had hidden in a barn outside Prague. His father was liberated—barely—from Buchenwald. My grandmother passed away when I was an infant, but I remember brushing my fingers along the numbers on my grandfather's leathery arm, trying to feel the numbers.

My father would flip his shit if he found out I was getting a tattoo.

Looking through the artwork, I wanted to cry. It could have been the margaritas or that the art was that inspirational. That beautiful. Why did people feel the need to permanently brand something on themselves? What experiences led to this? Or, what lack of experience? I couldn't imagine that people singed these images onto their skin. Forever. I knew what that felt like, to have something under your skin you couldn't remove. No scrub, no wishing would do the trick. You were branded.

"I can do a custom drawing for you, if you want," Raine said.

It hurt. Despite being tipsy, and despite what many people said; it fucking hurt. Not as badly as that night with the bartender in the closet, crying all the while as he pushed and didn't listen, and, well, we all know that story. Mine was only one of an unfortunate anthology of women's stories in closets—but it was my own.

Two weeks later, the ink still hadn't dried. In the end, I'd chosen a flower. Specifically, I'd selected a Venus flytrap. *Dionaea muscipula.* Held by a thin stem in a terra-cotta pot, two closed green lobes, and one pried open by an invisible enemy, trigger hairs depicted like teeth. Now, the weeping ink made it look like the Venus flytrap was crying.

Isn't it funny how a thing can represent both the goddess of love and also death? Not funny in a ha-ha way. Does something have to die before we can love? It's all mythology. Is that what our stories become? Myths? If we let them. But on the other hand, Venus doesn't only represent love. Sometimes, Venus represents sex. Sometimes, it's only about sex. Violent, unwanted, burning sex.

It was the High Holidays. The one time of year synagogues were filled to capacity: rooms opened up, extra chairs fitted into every corner. Even if at no other time, people observed during the High Holidays. First is Rosh Hashanah, the beginning of the Jewish new year, and the holidays stretch on for weeks after that. I stopped going to synagogue years ago, leaving my father to go alone, refusing to fill in for my mother's absence. I couldn't bear one more droning sermon. One more up-down-up workout in ill-fitting shoes and scratchy stockings. I couldn't bear to falsely bang my chest and ask forgiveness of people who wouldn't hear me, or from a God I wasn't sure I believed in. But my father still invited me to his apartment for holiday dinners. And I went. Brisket and challah for Rosh Hashanah. Bagels and lox for the break-fast meal that signals the end of Yom Kippur. Brisket, again, and even more wine for the Passover seders.

I'd thought I'd get out of Rosh Hashanah dinner this year. I've never been able to keep anything from my father. I'd only kept the tattoo a secret for a few months thus far, and had done so by declining invitations to my father's house. Begging away when he needed someone to drive him for his cataract surgery. Claiming to be sick when he needed help hanging a new painting. It was early September in New York City, and still eighty-something degrees outside. My father always got on my case when he saw that my summer wardrobe included sleeveless tops. *A little modesty,* he'd implore. He enjoyed a good shrimp cocktail or BLT—*who doesn't?* he'd say—but he was still influenced by his Orthodox upbringing and played the role of meddling mishpachah. Most of the time, it was endearing. But I knew that if I showed up with long sleeves in the warm weather, he would wonder what was up. My tattoo, and my bruised self, stayed away. Then, I accepted my father's invitation to Rosh Hashanah dinner. I decided to bring a sweater to throw on even if it caused suspicion—to hide the tattoo, hide what had happened, hide myself.

A light breeze triggered my plant's fine hairs, caused the mouth to snap shut. "I understand. I know," I whispered to the creature on my arm. In a city like New York, someone talking to their arm wasn't so strange. "You keep as closed up as you want, for however long you want."

I got off the bus two stops early. I passed the club where it happened—the desecration, *my* desecration. It was closed. As it would be; it was two o'clock in the afternoon. I had gone to the bar alone that night. I asked for my first drink, on the rocks, and turned in circles on the bar stool until I grew dizzy. Later, lying prone in a booth, I warbled along to a Rihanna remix with some post-grad sorority sisters. With them I had my fourth and fifth drinks, and we stumbled out into the bleak night together, me without settling my tab. The bartender came after me, insisted I come back inside. The sisters walked off, their hair straight and perfect, shining in the light from the streetlamps above. I followed the bartender back into the bar, which had emptied of patrons. Empty, it smelled of maraschino cherries and stale beer, occasional whiffs of sharp cologne. *Here, come in here*, he said, *we can settle your tab*. I said I wanted to get home. My boyfriend was waiting, I said. *You have to settle your tab, missy.*

Now, in the light of day, the club was a place of ghosts.

I brought my hand to my arm. Looking down, a green smear where my flytrap had mottled my skin. Only the terra-cotta planter and the teeth of the thing remained. I'd have to go back to the tattoo shop. Talk to Raine. Get it redone. Did I really want to go through that pain again?

As I approached the building that had housed Raine's studio, I saw that it, too, was closed. A For Lease sign hung in the front window. The curtains were drawn; there was no indication the storefront had been occupied recently. At the door, a pile of circulars blew in the wind: a sale on soda at the Food Emporium, discounts on plumbing.

I carried on down the street and turned north, bewildered at the shop's absence. A couple blocks farther, I entered the huddled masses of the city. I'd intended to get on the train at Union Square, but walked right past the station entrance and toward the Greenmarket stalls. Kale and jellies and apples, piled high. Women dressed in shorts and espadrilles tried to hold on to the remnants of summer. Wicker baskets and old-fashioned bicycles circled the tables, as though I were at a country market and not in the middle of Manhattan. I stopped at a table selling local honey. Small glass jars and delicate plastic straws filled with the sticky amber covered the gingham-clothed table. A small felt bee tethered by pipe cleaners wobbled in the breeze. It stared at me, accusing. I wavered between wildflower and blackberry but ultimately settled on a different one, clover.

It was clover that had filled my childhood lawn. A weed that my father refused to cut or mow or kill. It brought bees, he'd said. Like this was a good thing. *Bees sting*, I'd whine. *The important things always do*, he'd reply. Even I had to admit the white flowers that dotted our grass every spring and fall did look pretty. A few tables up, I selected some apples so burnished and shiny, they looked fake. I would bring apples and honey to my father's house for Rosh Hashanah. Tradition. Maybe that would make my secrets easier to bear.

A gust of wind shook the stalls' shelters. A few paper signs took flight. Thick drops of rain came. It wasn't a gradual storm. It announced itself upon arrival, booming—the voice of God, the *Daily News* would report the next day. As others fled to the nearest subway entrance, I headed up Park Avenue, determined to walk all the way to 71st. Rain be damned, it felt like what I imagined a baptism did. Cool. Clean.

It wasn't long before the paper bag holding the apples gave way and nearly dissolved, leaving me to balance my purchases in my arms. I shoved the honey straws and a few of the apples in my purse, but the leather satchel could only fit so much. I watched as the rain spattered onto my arm, further smudging my tattoo. Smears of green, tendrils of color wept along my skin. Later, I'd learn one of the honey straws had split open inside my bag. I'd never get its sweet stickiness out completely.

With water between my toes and apples in my arms, I arrived at my father's prewar building. Under the awning, I paused, collecting myself. I tugged on my wet sweater and watched the rain. Taxis whished by, dodging delivery trucks, bike messengers, and jaywalking pedestrians. Honks and distant sirens and the rain, the music of the city. A taxi with a lit sign approached a block away. I could get in, take it to Port Authority. Leave the city. I walked toward the curb, maneuvering all my things into one arm as I lifted my hand to call the taxi. I would leave. As easy as that, I would go home.

"Good to see you! Your father is preparing a feast; I can smell it!" Martin the doorman said to me from behind. The taxi had slowed but now I lowered my arm, shook my head, turned. The taxi sped off, displacing a puddle of water, soaking my feet.

I smiled, defeated, and followed Martin inside. My shoes squeaked as I walked along the slick floor toward the elevator, which had a door to open manually before the automatic elevator door slid open. A hand pushed the door open for me as I stepped into the closet-like space. I nodded to Barney and he pressed nine. He and my father played cards together and occasionally went to the movies at senior discount rates. He'd been the elevator operator for the building for over thirty years; after we moved here from the suburbs when my mom died, he became like an uncle to me. Today, I said nothing. The cramped elevator was air-conditioned, and I shivered. I sniffled. When the elevator reached the ninth floor, I stepped off. Seven doors lined the dimly lit hallway, two of which were stairwell entries. The other five were apartments. The door farthest down the hall belonged to my father. It felt very far away. I slushed down the time-flattened carpet. I glanced at the mezuzah affixed to the doorframe. This was the door to my father's house. To his life. To my life—to the life I used to know. Protected by God or superstition or love; it was all murky now. I pulled at my sleeves to hide my scars; though the sweater was soaked, its weight felt right.

My father came to the door, even though he'd left it open; Martin had called up to let him know I'd arrived. My father ushered me in like he hadn't seen me in ages and as though he were already an old man: stooped, smiling with his crow's feet.

"Come in, come in," he said.

"I brought apples." I held my hands out. Two of them fell to the floor and rolled into the living room.

"So you did. They're perfect." He gathered the ones on the floor and together we moved back into the kitchen where the smell of stewing beef and onions swirled in the air. I went to my old bedroom and changed clothes. Something dry. Something modest. In an oversized sweatshirt, I returned to the kitchen. After assessing me for a minute, my father handed me a grater and a pile of carrots. I set to work. Grating and grating, at first

THE INK THAT DOESN'T DRY   87

slowly, deliberately. Then I pushed the carrot harder and faster, sensing the fragments dropping onto the plate below, piling up. I kept going, down to the tips of the vegetable, my knuckles cramping, until the grater met my skin. At my fingertips, the fine blades on the grater bit in. Drew blood.

My father noticed. "Sarah, honey, be careful there." I ran my hand under the faucet and rinsed the grater.

"Dad?"

"Yes?" he asked, but didn't look up from tasting the beef gravy. His back was curved like he was protecting the pot. He took such care in making a perfect gravy, a perfect meal, for just the two of us. A burgundy tablecloth with a fine filigree of gold lay on the table, set with the special china—the dishes from my parents' wedding, the ones with the tiny roses at the center. Silver forks and spoons lay atop linen napkins. Goblets for water and wine sat behind the dishes. Unlit but ready candlesticks stood sentinel over the table. The brisket had been braising for hours.

"Never mind." I just couldn't. He had worked so hard. I didn't want to ruin it.

He licked the gravy from the sides of his mouth. "A little fatty, but then it stays on the lips longer, right?"

"Yeah," I said, and went back to grating. My shirtsleeves were a little too long, and brushed the pile of shredded carrots. I hiked the sleeve back, just slightly.

"How's the weather?" my father asked. As if he couldn't see from the windows. It was still pouring. "They say this global warming is going to wreak havoc all over. Heat waves in winter. Snow in spring. That sort of thing."

"It's already happening, Dad."

"Change is hard. It can be a result of something bad, or it can be the start of something good," he continued. He was still trundling around the small kitchen, attending to his pots and pans.

"What do I do with these?" I asked. The pile of carrots had been reduced to a haystack.

"Taste one," he said.

"Why? It's just carrot."

"Always taste your food while you're cooking."

"Yup, tastes like carrot," I said, scooping a pile of shreds into my mouth.

"Isn't it funny with things like that? You completely change a thing and it's still the same." He cut a cube of butter into a pan and swirled it around. As it melted, he pointed for me to put the carrots in. I did.

"I mean, we cook, we cut, we julienne and dice and cube and, in the end, it still tastes the same," he went on. He didn't say any more and we finished making the tzimmes and poured the warm, sweet carrots into a serving dish.

At the table, he sang the blessing over the food and the wine. It was beautiful, this archaic language that no one in my circle of friends knew. These prayers were so familiar to me, I could utter them in my sleep. I rarely sang along, though, allowing my father to hold the melody. In the silence of the night, with only muffled street sounds below, my father sang to me. When he reached the shehecheyanu, I opened my mouth. I allowed the words I had learned in Hebrew school to float out. With my eyes closed I could still see the candles my father had just lit.

"Shehecheyanu v'kiyimanu v'higi'anu laz'man hazeh," we sang together.

"Blessed are you, Lord our God, king of the universe, who has granted us life, sustained us, and enabled us to reach this occasion," my father translated.

After the meal, I went to wash my hands. As I lathered the soap—lavender and honey, the bottle said—I pushed my sleeves up. I brushed and caressed my arms, feeling my skin, every pore, every fine hair that was mine and only mine. The soap covered the tattoo in perfectly circular bubbles. The Venus flytrap slowly disappeared, so that when I dried off my arms, there was nothing but a small spine—a tooth, so tiny you'd think it was just a birthmark.

But with that little tooth remained an occasional faint pain that I rubbed sometimes, usually when I was cold or scared. I always know it's there. I think it will always be there. It will stay a part of me, something I can't fully erase. One day, I might forget all about the tiny tooth on my arm, letting it become just another mark on this lifelong body. I might forget. But I probably won't.

Domestic Appliance

Out in the suburbs, in a newly renovated rambler, in a granite-countered kitchen, in a stainless steel refrigerator, the kind that gives you ice and water from its door, lived a young woman. She couldn't recall how she came to live in the refrigerator, and she couldn't recall any life not lived inside of it. She woke up one day on a stick of butter; it had grown soft where her body rested, indentations of female hips and waist. Her feet almost reached the end of the stick. She was seven tablespoons of person.

It was a nice refrigerator, as fridges go. Fresh produce, rotating bottles of white wine and six-packs of beer, Friday-night Chinese takeout containers, marinating beef, an open box of baking soda. Rarely did anything expire.

When the fridge opened, the woman hid behind the milk, ducked into the egg carton, or sidled up to the pickle jar. A few pickles, peppercorns, and slivers of onion floated in the briny juice, dancing around each other to music she could not hear. She stared into the jar for hours. The light in the refrigerator was dull and gray, but it was enough to keep her from complete darkness. For sustenance, she would nibble on cheese, like a mouse. Other times, she'd pull open the side of a yogurt and slurp its strawberry cream. She avoided the condiments: Tabasco sauce, hoisin, capers crusty at the can's opening.

The woman was cold all the time.

Lunch sacks reading "Amos" in black marker, or, occasionally, "Dad" in a child's craggy print, were placed in the fridge daily by thin fingers with glossy nails. The woman always looked inside the paper bags. Usually, it was a sandwich, often tuna but sometimes PB&J, which the small woman found terribly endearing. Occasionally, there were dinner leftovers in plastic containers. Little red rounds of cheese, plastic bags filled with chips or chocolates. And, always, a folded-up note. Torn from a notebook, the pages were scribbled with the same thick marker that was used on the outside of the bag, and comprised a brief love letter: *Remember I love you!, You're the best!, Circle here: Y/N do you love me?* They were all very middle school, shaped into little paper footballs—that was what was so brilliant about them. The brutally manicured fingernails belied a sweet heart.

What did Amos look like, the fridge woman wondered? Months passed, and she became bolder. She watched Amos's comings and goings. His wife, it seemed, opened the door less and less. Amid the ins and outs of half-eaten pizza and deli meat, the fridge woman fell in love. Dark hairs spiraled on Amos's arms and hands. On his face, green eyes like the rind of a lime. Thick eyebrows, one always crunched up. He wore a smile whenever he surveyed the fridge. The tiny woman appreciated a man who found joy in small things.

One daydreaming morning, the fridge woman did not hide when Amos opened the fridge door. He reached for the ketchup absently and startled at the sight of her. He bent down and came eye to body with the small woman, who was leaning against a bottle of sriracha, collecting drips with her fingers and licking them, her minuscule lips puckering at the spice.

"Hello," Amos said. Too loud, for the tiny woman fell backward, but quickly got back up on her toothpick legs.

"Hi." She brushed her hair from her face.

"What are you doing in there?" Amos asked.

"Been assigned by the sanitary police. Things are starting to go bad. Did you know this blueberry yogurt expired two months ago?"

"I do know," he said. Frowned. He took the yogurt and tossed it in the trash behind him. "Gone. What else?"

"This applesauce. Hasn't expired yet, but it's all moldy at the top," she said, pointing to the jar. He took it, chucked it behind him.

"Okay, what else ya got?" The fridge woman was about to give up some fuzzy meat in tinfoil when Amos's wife came up behind him.

"Close the door," the wife said.

"Trying to figure out what to eat," Amos replied, not removing his eyes from the woman on the shelf.

"You're letting the cold out," his wife said.

"It's plenty cold out here," he said. The fridge woman snickered and from above Amos's head, a pale hand appeared on the door and slammed the door closed. The small woman was left alone on the shelf with the steady electric hum of the fridge and its dull, gray cold.

Amos began leaving the fridge woman things, dry foods—toast points, sandwich cookies, a cereal O she fashioned into a bracelet. She nibbled on it in the evening hours leading up to Amos's nighttime visits. *Midnight munchies,* he shouted to the wife in the other room. She shouted back that he'd get fat, and who would love him then?

The fridge woman and Amos both knew the answer. But it was too absurd. Too impractical. It was unreasonable for a full-sized adult to have a relationship with a seven-tablespoons-sized adult.

The wife, frustrated by the crumbs on the fridge's shelves, rebuked Amos. *Who do you think is going to clean this up?* So much anger over a minor crime. Amos began to leave behind his lunch sacks when he went to work. Eventually, the wife stopped putting notes in the lunch sacks. Then, she stopped making Amos lunch altogether.

After a time, it was only the wife who opened the fridge. Amos gone a day, then a week, then a month.

Depressed, the fridge woman drank from open mugs of beer and coffee gone rancid. The lettuce wilted, then became gooey, then turned to murky black liquid at the back of the fridge; the clear plastic box became a science experiment. She nibbled kernels of rice gone hard from barely eaten takeout. Both women did. Together, they shared the sordid remnants of the stainless-steel refrigerator.

The wife opened the fridge, stared inside; closed the fridge, taking out nothing. The wife stood in the cold of the fridge with red-rimmed eyes. The wife drank the juice from the pickle-less pickle jar; put the jar back. The wife scrubbed the produce drawer. The wife threw out the condiments.

She did not notice the woman in the fridge, who had few places left to hide. One day, the wife left the refrigerator door open. Just a little. The cold began to weep out. The tiny woman looked down to the wood floors below, outside. A powdery light came through the windows. She did not know it was the sun, but it was inviting. She thought to jump. She thought to make a run for it. But then the wife noticed her mistake and slammed the door shut, nearly catching the tiny woman's hair. The fridge woman fell back, and for days no one came again.

On the last remaining bottle of beer, the fridge woman pushed. With her back up against the glass, cold with condensation, she crunched her eyes, the veins in her neck straining. On the label, a dragon sat on a swing. Dangerous, wistful—both. She understood. She gave the bottle one more heave and it fell over with a metallic clunk. She tried to pry off the top. It was a twist-off. With her entire body she wound and wound. And then: a spill of beer. Glug glug glug came the amber liquid. The woman slipped to the shelf below. Opened her mouth to take it in, the deluge of ale inundating her. It was more than her small body could handle. She couldn't stop it. Struggling to breathe. Drowning. She fell to her knees, and then onto her back.

Amos returned. It would be only the one time; these things happen, he told his buddies. After sex with his soon-to-be ex-wife, Amos crept past her snoring body and went to the kitchen. It was nearly morning and gauzy light filtered through dirty windows. He went to the fridge. The internal ice machine released its uniform cubes. Fingerprints smudged the stainless-steel door.

Inside, he found her, minuscule mouth agape, arms mere fragile wisps. Sticky alcohol covered her body and the nearby shelves. He pinched her small body with his fingertips, resting her head on the pad of his pointer finger. Setting her in the kitchen sink, he cried. He could hear his almost-ex-wife's snoring from upstairs. It was muffled from this distance, but it still grinded. He pushed a finger on the small woman's chest. Blew a breath of air into her mouth, like blowing an eyelash off a fingertip. Push. Huff. Push. Huff. Her eyelids stuttered. Her lips twitched.

She coughed. Amber liquid fountained out of her, enough to fill a thimble. She opened her eyes and lifted her head. Recognized the great tendrils of wild arm hair first and lay her head back down. Amos placed her on a potholder, told her to hang on a minute.

He took a rag to clean the spilled beer. Wiped the countertops, too. He studied the toaster oven and microwave. There were no tiny women there. Were there always women in the corners and crevices in the world that directed life? Was their purpose to go unnoticed? But he had noticed her. Did this happen to other people? With a dishtowel and clean sponge, he made a bed for the small woman in a plastic storage container. He closed the refrigerator door and wiped his fingerprints from the stainless steel.

For the Dachshund Enthusiast

This is a message for the dachshund enthusiast who lives across the airshaft. It is the case, here in Manhattan, that we live in close quarters. On any given muggy New York day, my window is open. As is yours. The only thing between us is a fraction of diluted sunlight, the whir of a giant fan below, and an occasional pigeon that has lost its way. We might as well be roommates. So, I am quite familiar with your dogs, Harpo and Marx, and I am very sorry about Charlie Chaplin; it is true, he was part of the family.

I know you spend hours on the phone as a volunteer for New York Dachshund Rescue. You listen to people's stories and nod along and are silent until they are done. You then offer the kindest voice, a lilt that I had never heard before. I am amazed how many dogs go missing here in our city. Where do they go? You would think there would be packs of them, Pomeranians, terriers, dachshunds—compact, urban dogs—roaming Central Park, chasing the rollerbladers or begging at the kabob trucks. But, I must say, it's a wonderful service you provide; I don't mean to make light of it.

Recently, when your daughter was coming to visit, you cleaned your apartment from the back corners of the closet to the butter section of the fridge. I'm sorry that I watched. I was eating one of those microwaved meals, something that Louisa, my late wife, would have been horrified by. I watched long after I had finished eating, the sauce congealing in the plastic tray. I sat for such a time that I grew hungry again. You swished around like I hadn't seen you do before. Your auburn hair bounced at your chin; you wore the apron with the cherries. You tangoed with the vacuum cleaner. The astringent lemony scent had wafted over, making me feel as though my place was a hovel in comparison, thick with dust and cockroaches. Harpo and Marx could sense something was up. Your roasted chicken smelled divine, even from here.

When she phoned to say she would be late, you were so gentle. You petted Harpo's soft ears like they were a salve; it relaxed you, I could tell. When she phoned later, I could sense your irritation was growing. When she finally arrived and said she could only stay for twenty minutes because she had another engagement, your irritation turned to sadness. I don't think she noticed.

How are you, Mom? Really? she asked. You said things were fine and that you'd been attending lectures at the 92nd Street Y. That you occasionally saw Alice, though I've never seen anyone at your house. Maybe that's where you go on Wednesday mornings.

After your daughter left, you sat at the table with the teal tablecloth and ate your perfectly roasted chicken, the drumstick whole in your hand. I don't blame you. That's the best part of the bird. You picked prime pieces off and fed them to the dogs, bending low, for they are short animals. You didn't drop the meat onto the floor, as so many others would have done. You waited for them to take it carefully in their teeth.

I also once had a dog. Bess. A corgi. Also a low and long animal, she had difficulty jumping onto the couch, like your Charlie
Chaplin did. I've seen Harpo and Marx use each other for help
to get up on the sofa. They're impressive, these dogs of ours.
Aside from a magnet I was handed at the health clinic, Bess's
photograph is the only thing on my refrigerator. Memorialized
in black and white, though in life, her coat was a terrific copper. She was my lucky penny. As a young man, I found her—just
a puppy, in an alley—and took her home, thinking nothing of
where she had come from and marveling at my good fortune.

Bess was my first love, and I loved her fiercely. I know you
know something about that. Then came Louisa, who became my
wife, and we were a magnificent trio. The three of us shared a
small cottage on Lake George. It was entirely unlike life in the
city. The square footage wasn't all that different, but the way the
sky and trees reflected off the lake, the world felt limitless. We
moved to the city to be closer to Louisa's parents, and while I
couldn't say I loved the new pace of life, Bess flourished. Snowy
walks in Central Park, thousands of people to greet, children to
seduce in her ever-a-puppy way.

When the day came to put Bess down, I cried as I walked
along Broadway. I carried her limp body in my arms. At the time,
it was the most difficult moment of my life. We did what had to
be done with the help of a kind veterinarian over on 74th Street
who was willing to come in on a Sunday. After, Louisa had to
carry my soul and spirit back up Broadway, up the steep and
narrow stairs all the way to the fifth floor of our walk-up. She
tended my wounds, and slowly we continued with life, just the
two of us.

Later, I was unable to tend to Louisa as thoroughly as she
tended to me through my grief. Louisa didn't make it more

than ten years after the day we lost Bess. I like to think of them together, bounding into the shallows of the lake. It is always summer and it is always dusk where they are. Maybe Charlie Chaplin is there, too.

Listen to me going on and on. What I mean to say is, I'm sorry I was eavesdropping. I didn't mean to be a voyeur, unwelcome, a Peeping Tom. But I felt invited in by our closeness. Our proximity, a gift of such a crowded city. Your fragrant roasted meat brought to mind my Louisa in the kitchen, delicately slicing a brisket as though it were a filet mignon. Since that very first day of sweltering summer when you opened your window, you've allowed your spirit to drift out.

I feel like I am dancing with you when you play Tito Puente long into the evenings, when the square of sky above is peach, then copper like my Bess, then passes into the indigo of night. What I really mean to say is that you are welcome to visit anytime. Please bring Harpo and Marx. I will make spaghetti—no TV dinners for you—and you, bring your records. The breeze from our airshaft will cool the humid night and we will laugh and dance and maybe sing, and the dachshunds—squat and fat and loving us, always—will lie at our feet on the cool parquet floor. The hours will pass and you will forget entirely that I am a stranger.

Notice of Proposed Land Use Action

This is a notice to tell you that you will be removed from your house in sixty days. We understand it is the multigenerational home of your family, that your childhood heights and your mother's childhood heights and your grandfather's childhood heights are marked on the same doorframe. As are your brother's, and your sister's, and your two aunts'.

We understand you were born there; upstairs, in the second room on the right. That your mother labored for eleven hours and there you slithered onto the knotty pine floor, yowling. That the stains of your birth were covered by a round rug decorated with a ring of small red flowers and blue and orange curls. Rosemaling, they call it; your great-grandparents brought it over from Norway in 1927 along with a single suitcase and your soon-to-be-born grandfather. We know that sometimes your mother pulled up the rug and pressed her face to the stain when you were a teenager. When you told her you hated her and slammed doors and had sex in the laundry room but denied it even though she found condoms in the dryer.

After your sister was hit by a car while chasing an escaped tetherball, and after she lay pretty and cold at the funeral home up the block, and after she was deposited into the ground, your mother rested her head on the hard floors again. For hours at a time, she spread her soft body on the kitchen linoleum and on the original-to-the-house hexagonal tiles of the bathroom. They were cold, still are, and could turn a hot flush into something not unlike pain when needed.

We will be demolishing everything left inside, so you better make sure you take everything you want. That Ouija board under the floorboards of your bedroom closet? That, too. Otherwise we will take any ghosts and phantoms who linger and crush them down into the sediment of the earth. Above, we will build rectangular townhouses constructed like LEGO bricks with brightly colored doors. Ochre or sunbeam or vermillion—buyer's choice. The ghosts—your ghosts—they can float down another hallway, another street. They'll follow you wherever you go.

You should think about digging up your sweet mutt, Larry, with the one floppy ear and the one Doberman ear, and also the many dead gerbils you buried in the yard. We will be placing large four-by-four paving stones down to create a patio; no need for grass—we want these homes to be low-maintenance. The grill will go over there, and a raised garden bed or two can go over here. The new residents will grow peppers and tomatoes and beets. They will reach into the loamy dirt and pull out organic meals and proclaim: *It came from our very own garden! With my own two hands! Can you believe it?* Their friends will shake their heads, hand off a can of local IPA, and say, *No, we can't.*

You may also want to dig up the time capsule you planted when you were eight. We know it was meant to be opened in twenty-three years, but no harm in pulling it out a little early. Bet you can get good money for the Mary Lou Retton Wheaties box and that Paddington collectible bear, even with the ear chewed—you were such a nervous child. Take out the love poem you wrote to the squirrels, the letters from your Japanese pen pal, the Polaroids of you and your little sister dressed as the Doublemint twins, and the postcard that reads: *Dear Sugar, The Holy Land sure is holy! I keep falling into them left and right! Can't wait to see you. Love, Grandpa.* Recycle them, perhaps.

But first, we are going to erect this chain-link fence. When the weeds grow high and hide the house in its shadows, it will be time for the Department of Planning and Development to go in and conduct an environmental review. Is it safe, is there lead, the water levels, and all that.

See that billboard? That's one of ours. "Every act of creation is first an act of destruction." It's a quote from Picasso. It's supposed to make you feel good about this. Don't you feel good?

Approval has been received. We're sorry about the economy. That recession hit hard, didn't it? Anyway, the project will go ahead as planned. And thank you. Really. You are an integral part of seeing this plan come to fruition. You are part of this creation. Your life, your entire life, we are indebted to.

When you stuck your fingers into the knotty wood floors, when you hid under the sink with the cleaning supplies you thought smelled of oranges and love, when you snuck up onto the roof to read Encyclopedia Brown or Goosebumps during the Fourth of July barbeques, you knew exactly where to place your feet to climb higher and higher, and where you could sit and still get a good view of cousins and friends eating burgers and coleslaw, and you hummed along as they sang wonky versions of "The Star-Spangled Banner," making up their own lyrics like it was a contest. Your father always saved you a plate. Hot dog, no bun, potato chips, and a tangy pile of ketchup. Don't let us destroy those memories. Take them when you go.

The mantel, the cupboards, the doorknobs, the doors—all of it will be auctioned off or brought to one of those salvage warehouse stores. People love period details.

About the chimney. When you were six, you climbed up it from the inside to check that it was clear for Santa. When you got stuck there for two hours, your brother tossed fruit roll-ups and jellybeans from above to keep you calm. Such a nice brother. Are you still close? Anyway, the chimney will be the first to go. It holds the entire structure up.

When the damp enters through those knotty floorboards and you think you can't drive by the old, sodden family home once more without killing yourself, it'll be gone. Just like that. An empty lot of tall yellow grass, a few pieces of siding here, a brick there. Maybe you think you see the rocking chair where you rocked your baby sister every night and sang to her that she had the whole world in her hands, but you don't. The ghosts, the pine floors, the rug, the stain, the hexagonal tiles—it's all gone.

Minutes later, it will seem, our beautiful modern townhouses will be up in its place. Bright and airy and filled with young families from out of town. We will be able to build eight townhouses on this lot. Eight! Each with a one-car garage and parking pad. LEED certified, all that. Silver. Gold. Platinum. Whichever is the best.

We believe sustainability is key to the future.

This Warm and Breathing Thing

Under the blitzing, buzzing lights and above the flecked, shiny flooring reflecting the blitzing and buzzing yellow lights, I sit and wait. Every time I move, the pleather and metal seat creaks and squeals. Then, everyone in the room looks up, assessing where the sound came from. It is the most interesting thing happening in the room. We are all sitting, and we are all waiting.

In the corner, runner-up for most interesting thing, is an old woman needlepointing. In and out go the thin threads; she pulls and yanks and uses her teeth. She has a tiny pair of scissors that occasionally get taken from a basket. Snip, snip. Even from across the room I can tell they're sharp. She doesn't look up. Punch and pull. Punch and pull.

Beyond the door, there is so much happening of interest. A flurry of tests and fluids, imaging and bodies cracking under pressure. Interesting. Tragic. Hopeful. Depressing. Miraculous. Hopeless.

I'm concerned about the salmon I left in the skillet on the stove. I turned the stove off—of that I am sure. Will I ever get home? And when I do, with all the time elapsed and all that has happened, will that salmon have gone moldy and embedded its low-tide sea stink into the curtains? Will I have to move? Will I have to get rid of everything?

I have to go to the bathroom, but I don't want to miss it. Anything. I am also hungry. Do I buy a bag of Combos? It's leaning against the window of the vending machine as if begging me. As if I could just shake the machine and it would fall and I wouldn't have to pay for it at all.

The fish will start to stink. It had already smelled up the house as I cooked. It was Copper River salmon. Short season. Expensive. Pinkety pink. It was our anniversary and Brendan had to work late so it was 9 P.M. and I was cooking and the cat came around the corner at the aroma and I fed it canned meat they call pâté. I was preparing a fine meal for us, one we would eat together with wine and the dimmer down low and the local dance station playing on our old kitchen radio.

There were vegetables roasting in the oven. Cauliflower—that also stinks when it cooks. Why do we even eat such things? Pulled the baking dish out, at first forgetting an oven mitt and nearly burning my fingers. Switched that off, too. I am pleased with my foresight to turn these things off—things that could burn down our house. If we let it.

As I'd prepared, the lemon had stung the tiny cracks in my hands. I have eczema and I forget this every time. Acid burns. Even now, hours later, my hands are splotched with tiny red dots like an expressionist painting.

A doctor comes in on white sneakers. We all look up. He walks toward one man. Two children, about seven and ten years old, are sitting on the floor by his feet, reading. They belong to the man, the children. He listens to the secret treasures the doctor is imparting. He pulls his son and daughter up by their collars. They've grown lethargic in the wait. I'd noticed them turning pages of their books, slowly—too slowly. They are led out of the waiting room, the doctor's hand on the man's shoulder. The boy and girl trail behind.

The needlepointer still does not look up. One of the kids has left their book under a chair. I wait to see if they return. The clock tick tick ticks. I watch the second hand and I am sure it moves backward before moving forward again. I dive for the book, then return to my seat without looking at the others in the room. It looks old, worn, used. The pages are yellowed. I recognize the series from my own childhood. There is scrawl inside. Red pen, block lettering. Smiley faces. Doodles. I return to the first page and start to read.

Four pages in, I get a paper cut and am surprised the soft old paper has it in it to still cause such pain. I suck the wound, small, barely visible but painful. It'll pass, I know.

At 9:07 P.M. I got a call. I thought it would be Brendan saying he was going to be late. But it was a bland-sounding woman calling from Hartland General and could I please come in as soon as possible? But first she asked if I was in fact Jenna Bartlett and I said yes, yes I am who wants to know, and are you calling about Brendan? She said she was but couldn't say more and could I please come down to Hartland General as soon as possible Mrs. Bartlett, thank you, and then she hung up and I was left with a dial tone that sounded like something out of 1990, when Brendan and I met. We were only fourteen then, and we'd crank-called people all night. We'd eaten Pop-Tarts and grapes and orange soda until we burped. He didn't kiss me that night. Didn't for over a decade, in fact.

I notice Orange Crush is an option in the other vending machine. The people in the room have helped themselves to many cups of steaming hot coffee (or maybe cocoa) from the third and final machine, something I didn't even know they made anymore, the hot-drink vending machines, that is. I reach for my wallet tucked deep into my tote bag. There, I find a couple of rumpled soft-like-laundry dollar bills and feed one to the machine. It comes right back out. I flatten the corners and try again but it is again spit out. I try another bill. Rejected. Another. I kick at the machine. *Fuck*, I say as the bill slips like a feather to the ground. Fuck.

"Here, let me help you," says a voice. I turn and see the needle-pointer. She is taller than I'd have thought, about my height—five eight. Her thin hair was clearly once coiffed, but it's fallen and the dyed dark strands cannot conceal her scalp. It looks so vulnerable there, under the pretense of youth. The woman expertly pushes the bill against the window of the machine, slowly running her hand over every crease and fault. She then feeds the machine. "What would you like?" I want to say Diet Coke, as if that somehow is more acceptable, but I push the button for Orange Crush and it rattles down the machine and out. I'll have to wait to open it; I don't want it to blow up everywhere.

"Thanks," I say and pull a smile onto my face, sure I look like a carnival's funhouse clown. She opens her mouth to say something more; I can tell she wants to trade stories. She left her needlepoint on her chair. I can see she has stitched the outline of a person with a long neck and the beginning of a cap of dark hair, but the rest isn't filled in yet. Perhaps it is this woman when she was younger. Perhaps not. She wears a wedding ring but no one else is with her here. She isn't checking a cell phone. She doesn't seem impatient. Her eyes are pale gray in that probably once-blue way. Thin hints of lipstick fill the lines around her lips but her lips themselves are the color of the rest of her skin.

"Want a drink?" I offer.

"Gave up soda thirty years ago," she says. "Along with ciga-rettes." She sounds like a hot-air balloon full of regrets and I can almost hear the beginning of the leaking air. "Fat lot of good that's done me."

"Sorry," I say, because I can't think of what else to say and I don't want to hear her story. I think I may know it anyway, pretty much. I crack the tab of the soda too soon and it fizzes and fuzzes with foam. I quickly bring it to my mouth and catch the sweetness. "Thanks again," I say and sit back in my chair. She likewise resumes her old spot across the room, resumes her needlepoint work. I stare at the clock as if that will make time go faster.

My hands have become sticky from the soda can. I should wash them. The bathroom is out of this room and down the hall-way, and I do still have to go, but it is a long journey and things could be missed so I toss the can in the recycling bin and lick my fingers one by one. Another time this might have been sexual, coy. I wipe my hands along my winter parka, which I still have on, that I wear despite it being early spring. I can't bring myself to think I'll be staying long or that I don't need the warmth.

I married Brendan when we were both thirty-four, twenty years after that night of crank phone calls. We were on-again, off-again friends, went to different colleges, and had gone our separate ways, but we met again at a high school reunion at a bar on a Sunday at 3 P.M. Drunk and not wanting to walk into the daylight, we made out in a bathroom stall and laughed at the routine the cheerleaders put on. They had planned it and in the wake of flash mobs and coordinated wedding dances, they danced to "Hey Mickey" and made a human pyramid that even-tually fell, and while Rachel Burton nursed an injured wrist, everyone laughed and laughed and drank some more. *Oh, the good old days*, Rachel's former beau and football MVP Mark said. Rachel eventually made a sling out of a white cloth napkin. Rachel, at that point, had four children and a pastor husband in an indeterminate sect of Christianity. She wore a long floral skirt and we think this is why she fell off the pyramid: wrong outfit. I heard she has had four more children and lives in Idaho now. Mark died on September 11, 2001. He was a firefighter. We all chipped in a few dollars to send to his wife, to help with the grief.

Brendan and I dated for years before he finally proposed and we married on the grounds of a barn. The wedding was supposed to be shabby chic, but ended up more shabby than chic. And it rained. But we had a great time. We laughed and drank and looked into the night like we had all the time in the world until morning.

We decided no kids. We decided to run marathons together. We decided to live in a condo along a lake that had an extra bedroom but we never had any guests.

Last summer I had stopped taking the pill. Wasn't I too old, anyway? *Aren't we past this?* Brendan had asked. And then we were celebrating our anniversary two days later and we still didn't talk about it and I was making his favorite meal and we would talk about it and revel in the change of plans and it would all be great and I would share my love of reading with her and we would love him so, so much. Would she love salmon? I hope he isn't allergic to cats. Would I have to deliver via C-section? Could we have a home birth? A water birth? Talk and talk and talk, he said, as I went through our options and he flipped another page of his economics magazine. He said you just talk and talk and talk.

So, I said nothing.

A man in pink scrubs comes in and whispers to the needle-pointer. She shoves all her things into the basket and follows him very closely, almost stepping on his heels. She nods at me and pulls her mouth thin. I smile back and blink several times as if trying to send her a message via Morse code. I don't know what I'm saying. A couple minutes later, she comes back in and hands me her embroidery hoop and basket, carefully indicating where the needle is stuck so I don't hurt myself.

"You're going to want to have something to do with your hands," she says and slips back out of the room. I look at the image, which she has made significant progress on. There's a sun in the top corner. The woman has the same long black hair I do, though my hair is currently up in a bun, the same lilac scarf, glasses. A cat rests curled by her side.

I tuck the children's book into my purse to save for my future reader. Will someone set up one of those personalized fundraising pages for me? At least we have the extra bedroom.

The clock tick tick ticks.

The surgery went well.

We had a few hiccups . . .

Good news . . .

I'm sorry to say . . .

Well, the good news is . . .

Your Bob is a fighter.

She's asking for you.

He's asking for you.

She came through.

I text my neighbor to ask if she can feed the cat. Tell her Brendan is in the hospital. I had woken her up. She said yes, of course. Anything else, she asks. I say no and she says she will pray for Brendan. I don't tell her it's too late, probably, and that she should pray for me instead.

Half an hour later, I realize I've forgotten to ask my neighbor to put away the salmon. I don't want to bother her further; it's past midnight. The house will smell like a low-running creek. Like cat food gone bad or the wretched section of the local grocery store displaying previously frozen shrimp and crab legs.

The clock tick tick ticks.

I'm starting to get uncomfortable after that soda. I want to go to the bathroom but what if they come right then? What if I miss the doctor and the update? I wonder, if I'm not there to receive the news, did it really happen or could Brendan still be in that magical space where he is alive to me. I cross my legs. I uncross them, let my shoes dangle and then fall off, and wrap my legs to sit cross-legged. I tie my scarf tighter around my neck and look down at the basket of needlepoint supplies. I'm not good at crafts. Will I never see that old woman again? I contemplate leaving the basket behind when it's time for me to go, but I know I won't.

The seat creaks again with every movement, but there is no one else left to hear it. They have come for everyone else. I hear the distant PA and talking just outside the door. Rain pings on the windows and I realize this whole time I could've been looking outside, studying something, who knows what, something that is outside this room, something uncontrollable, the weather, the sunset, the night's descent. That's it. I'm going. I stand to go to the bathroom, but as I do, the door swings open and I see a white sneakered foot.

At home I notice the salmon and vegetables are gone. The neighbor has cleaned the frying pan and scrubbed the char from the baking dish and they're now resting in the drying rack. I open the trash, but can't find the remnants of the meal. The house doesn't smell like salmon and I am relieved beyond measure. I spy small flakes of pink in the cat's bowl and I am okay with this. She enjoyed it, I'm sure, this small luxury. Sammy never jumps on counters; she is so well behaved.

I take out my contacts with shaky hands, let my hair down, and wind the scarf back around my neck in the apartment's chill. Our bedroom is unbearable so I go sit on the couch in the dark. A little light from outside—a streetlight, the moon—gets in, so it's not entirely dark, though it feels like it is. It will be morning soon. The cat comes in and meows, stretches her back and claws the couch before hopping up and settling beside me. I stroke her with trembling hands and she begins her windup purr, vibrating her body next to mine. I burp, from the soda. I see the collected anniversary cards we'd received and gave to each other in the morning. It's a pile of brightly colored envelopes: pink, orange, cornflower blue.

I will take up embroidery. I will hang this image on the wall, the gift from the older woman. I will see the sun in the morning. I will feed the cat. I will cry and cry and cry and then the sun will come up again. It feels so good, to be next to this warm and breathing thing.

The Potluck

The neighborhood potluck was in one week. Bright multicolored flyers were stapled to telephone poles and slipped under doors despite No Soliciting signs. On screens, commercials with glassy-eyed government officials in denim overalls eating out of wicker picnic baskets asking: *Is your family recipe the recipe you can't live without?* There hadn't been a potluck in ten years. It was something designed only to be as often as necessary.

Mrs. Court hung out her meat a month in advance. To fully dry, the jerky required zero to little humidity, so our arid climate offered the best environment, save for a kiln, and Mrs. Court had long abandoned her pottery. Too gratuitous, she thought, after her last child was gone. She rubbed the leathery strip with her withered fingers. Just about the texture of an old belt. In seven more days, it'd be perfect. She lamented how her husband couldn't see the way she had expertly seasoned the meat. Salt, pepper, mustard seed, clove, cinnamon, cayenne, all in equal measure. But it had been decided this would be his year.

His year to represent the A-frame green house on the corner.

The neighborhood had an abundance of children. That much was necessary for the offering, of course. In the off-years—the years the potluck didn't take place—the streets teemed with happy laughter. Bikes careened down the hill of Jackson Lane, skinned knees were collected like trading cards, teenage drama was relayed into cell phones—all under the protective watch of parents who had affairs with the schoolteachers.

But the adults always had it hanging over their heads. They remembered potlucks from their childhood, the feigned glee when the judges proclaimed their family's dish the best. They never came home with leftovers. Take it, they'd say. We don't want it anymore.

In the Anderson home, the shoddiest rambler filled with the happiest kids, six of them, all under ten, the air was electric. Joan and Mark settled into their full-size bed. Far too small for their collective volume.

"We need to choose, honey. I know it's not easy," Mark said, wiping his glasses yet again. He leveled his eyes at the back of her neck. Wispy strands of her hair created the most beautiful whorl. He moved in closer to press his lips to it, but she turned and her forehead smacked his chin.

"Jesus, Joan," and all the softness left the room. "We just have to do it. Names in a hat. Or we can just pick Lucas. He's barely three months. He wouldn't know the difference. We can just . . ."

"What?" Joan seethed. "Go on like before? Pretend he never even existed?"

"No. No," Mark said.

"Like those eighteen hours of labor and the surgery and NICU and the other surgery and the colic, just didn't fucking happen?" The baby started to cry in the nursery. Milk sprung from Joan's breasts as if they, too, were weeping.

"Okay, so how about Olivia? She's always such a pain." Mark was going for levity, but . . .

Joan and Mark ended up choosing the baby, telling the other children that Jesus wanted Lucas all to himself. Joan scribbled a list of ingredients and Mark took the rest of the kids to the grocery store to get them, allowing Joan some time alone. She took a bath—scalding hot—and pushed and pushed until she herself choked and vomited. When Mark returned, they worked together silently in the kitchen. They'd decided to make the dish in advance. It got better as it marinated, allowing time for the flavors to really meld together.

Up and down the block, and the block over, and two blocks from there, it was much the same. As the potluck approached, families grew tighter, smaller, more grim. Barbeques burped their charred meaty smells. Even though the weather was getting warmer, the sun inviting children to play, the people of the neighborhood stayed inside. Hoped their sacrifice would be enough. Tasted and tested and tried to think of the judges' palates.

Old Mr. Hudson hated anything too spicy. Daphne Hull ate it all, like that guy on television; she was game for anything. Indeed, she was the daughter of the neighborhood board president. Of course she was game. She would never be considered real game, anyway, thanks to her stature in the community. Cree Crabapple seemed only to like Italian dishes. Marinaras and ragus and Bolognese would all be popular at this year's potluck.

The night before, prayers were said. Even those that didn't believe, prayed. To Jesus, to Jehovah, to Allah, to Gaia. To long-dead grandparents and to the recently deceased. They prayed on their knees in the shower with their eyes closed and with their eyes glazed open in front of the oven. It was a night of a thousand suicides.

On baseball field No. 3 at Higgins Park, a long table covered in a red-and-white gingham tablecloth was lined with casserole-filled Pyrex, salads with fruit and other accoutrement, slow cookers with meatballs, serving utensils laid out next to the bowls like wounded soldiers, and white paper napkins waving in the breeze like so much surrender.

The three judges sat on the bleachers, a makeshift table set in front of them. Old Mr. Hudson tucked a napkin at his neck, which was endearing or gruesome, depending on how you looked at it. Daphne's nails were meticulously tended and glossy red. Cree looked frazzled with the attention, even though she had volunteered for the position.

We sat on the edges of the field, refusing to come any closer until we were called. Everyone was required to attend. We wanted to leave our children home, keep them away from the heinous tradition. But like so much violence on TV and in video games, it was inevitable, or so said the officials. *It is up to you if and when you explain it to them*, they said, and handed us pamphlets on how to broach the subject. There were websites on the dark web of ways to avoid the potluck draft, but the sites were often shut down as quickly as they'd shown up, their owners discovered and relocated immediately. For the safety of the neighborhood, we were told.

We watched from our great distance as the three judges were serenaded with dish after dish. They made genial remarks on the juiciness of this or the citrus notes of that into microphones that buzzed with feedback every twenty-one seconds. We counted. We were called up to present our own dish, explain its contents, our techniques, what we were going for. We blinked back tears, bit nails, and tightened our bowels as they sampled. Mr. Hudson with a bear paw grip on his fork. Daphne with a pinky up.

Cree with timid nibbles, finally truly understanding what she'd signed up for.

It was Mrs. Court's turn. Old Widow Court, as she would henceforth be named. Her dish was the least attractive. Dried-out, brownish-red strands on a gold-flecked Tiffany china platter. We could see from here the judges were apprehensive, as they picked with their fingers at the dish. But Daphne led the charge and placed the jerky between her blinding teeth. She chewed. Began to moan. For pleasure or disgust, we weren't yet sure. Then we watched as Mr. Hudson took a piece and shoved it in his maw. Cree followed and we watched as they chewed and they chewed and they chewed, masticating the last of Mr. Court.

"Winner!" Mr. Hudson cried out, despite not being able to determine the winner without conferring with his fellow judges.

Daphne patted his hand, nodded her head. "We will have to discuss this. But well done, Mrs. Court."

There were several dishes left, but it was clear none had as much culinary impact as Mrs. Court's jerky. She was branded the winner, but having no one else at home anymore, the prize was unnecessary. Single-occupant homes were exempt from the potluck anyway.

We hung our heads and with our pounding chests, we shuffled home, grateful for another decade without potlucks. Over the next months we devised ways to escape, hatched plans, whispered in the dark of night. But after a couple years, we fell lazily into the cadence of our small-town life, fooling ourselves about the lives we lived and the choices we had.

A flimsy blue ribbon decorated Mrs. Court's door. Journalists interviewed her. She briefly had a cooking show on the local cable channel. The spices she bought for her potluck dish expired, lost their flavor, turned rancid. Secretly, she had kept a small allotment of the crude preserved memory of her husband. In a plastic sandwich bag, it hung from a rusty nail above the kitchen sink. She said good morning and good night to it every day. Talked about their long-dead children and what they were not doing with grandchildren they did not have. Discussed the weather. Small talk, the kind that fits in your hand or in your pocket. The kind that's possible to lose if you drop it. The kind that says nothing, but says everything.

In My Sleep I Am Wounded

The itching begins at night. Fire on my scalp, ears aflame. I was dreaming about butterflies and barbed wire. I see the image: sky thick with thousands, if not millions, of butterflies—red, orange, blue—unmoving, suspended in air. I can't remember how the barbed wire figured in.

I scratch my scalp and pull away with skin beneath my fingernails. I feel but cannot see the skin, because it is night and dark. I walk to the bathroom, careful not to drop whatever it is I have found, although I have suspicions. For a moment, I rest my head on the doorframe, feel the mezuzah there—made of Jerusalem stone—a gift from my father. I reach out to touch it; we are not traditional and I do not believe in God or miracles.

I flip the light switch. Squint.

"Goddammit!"

There, wriggling under my nail, is a louse. I'm sure of it because as a child I had lice—to the chagrin of my perpetually cleaning mother—numerous times. I recognize the primordial creature, the semitransparent outline of its body, its abdominal undulations. It wants to suck more of my blood; I am keeping it from its life-sustaining task.

I am appalled. Disgusted. Surprised. I am not a teacher, nor do I have children. I did not try on any hats or rest my head on any stranger's pillows. How could I have contracted such a vile thing? My husband, still asleep in bed, will be horrified. His snores fill the air and the blowing HEPA air filter captures the sound and sucks it in.

I rinse my finger under the cold of the tap, watch the insect slide down into the drain. There are more, I know. And what? What then? It is two o'clock in the morning; am I to drive to the store, purchase a bottle of noxious lice-killing shampoo, and perform the whole ritual now? Smile sheepishly at the poor guy working the pharmacy's graveyard shift? Mumble something about a young afflicted daughter?

I remember my mother sitting outside on the porch with a fine-toothed comb. She'd pull and tug and tweeze my head, all the while muttering about the filth. I could wake my husband, but he has work in the morning. He must have contracted the vermin, too.

I'd have to tell him, of course.

Anyhow, it is winter, and too cold to sit barefoot on the splintered wooden stairs outside waiting for all the parasites and their eggs to be pulled from my head.

Just cut it off, my mother had said. *Cut it all off.*

The infestation has begun. I go to the kitchen for water, trying not to shake my head too much. No use getting the house thick with insects. I come back, sit on the toilet, hard and cold on my thighs. In my throat, the water is cool and metallic. I run my tongue along my gums, feel the bumpiness of my teeth. No, I have not bitten anything. There is no blood.

Surely, the creatures are in the folds of my sheets, the fibers of carpet. In the merino of my sweaters. In the strands of my DNA.

Not much I can do tonight, I decide. Back in bed I scratch and dig at my scalp. Every bite an insult. Every twitch a fear. I fight the horrible things by rubbing my head against the linen pillowcase until I fall asleep.

The butterflies do not return.

I wake on a wooden pallet and have no pillow. I am lying under a scrap of wool and it tears at me with every fitful move as I sleep. Pieces of yellowed grass cling to it, as does the pickled odor of decaying things. Outside I hear the pastoral sound of a rooster and then a gunshot. I remember I am in barrack E. Probably in the woods of Bavaria, only it's not the woods. Unless we are all creatures of the night, and wild. In a way, we are. I scratch at my head and find nothing below my shoulders. My hair has been cut. Shorn. Shaven. I can feel the uneven tufts of it. I feel at my wrists, my bones. Protruding clavicle. My legs are like kindling that won't catch a flame.

In my gut, hollow, something deep and thick—but also empty, and impossibly thin. The lice are not the enemy. They are only reminding me I have blood in my body. That I am alive at all.

I take a louse on my fingertip. Say hello. Call it Max. Place it back on my head.

And again I wake. And again. And again. And sometimes I am safe and other times I am not. Splinters of light through the window slats. Soft bedsheets tucked around my body. The lumbering snore of my husband. Then, the suck as that familiar sound is taken away.

In the bathroom, I look in the mirror. Sunlight hazes the room, all soft. I turn the overhead light on. I wince but need the brightness to see. My head does not itch. I scratch. Pull at my hair. When I take my hand away, I see only creamy flakes of dead skin. No spindly insect legs twitching in the air. The glass of water is on the counter, empty. Not a dream, exactly.

In the morning I tell my husband. Ask him to check my head. "Anything?" I ask. "Nothing," he says, bewildered. The phantom lice have left. They will not haunt me in the day. I reach up to scratch. He takes my hand into his own. Perhaps they will return, but they are not real. Not on my head. Today. This head. Now. Occasionally, I itch. I say, I know you are not far away. That you could come back anytime. You are just reminding me.

Solitaire

Of the accident: the speed limit was twenty-five. Natalie, mother and wife—mine—was in the crosswalk. His light was red. She was going to the pharmacy to pick up antibiotics for Maggie's ear infection. Verne—I learned his name later—scraped his forehead. One of Nat's leopard-print sneakers was found fifty feet away from her body. Verne was headed to the airport. Waves of her soft blond hair grew dark in a filthy, oily puddle—it had rained the night before. Verne said he was running late to pick someone up. She died on impact. Verne said the light was still yellow. Maggie never got the antibiotics; the infection went away on its own.

Maggie weaned instantly when my wife was killed by Verne's Prius driving fifty-six miles an hour. The baby—actually, she was more of a toddler now—was in a clingy phase. All Maggie wanted was for me to hold her, carry her, touch my body to hers. She pulled at my shirt. I knew what she wanted, but I was unable to express enough of anything to quell her need.

That was four months ago. Four months, one week, three days. Today, Maggie was eighteen months old. I decided to play fifty-two pickup with her. On the back of the cards was a photographic image of a saguaro cactus. A single three-pronged prickly thing lit up against a dark desert sky, so dark you could see your own reflection, in the photo that is. The real desert sky reflects back nothing. The cards were from a trip taken with Nat. Not just a trip. The trip. The last one. Unusual rainstorms turned our desert trip into a hotel-room, pregnant lady–sex, gin-rummy, room-service kind of vacation.

I thought a floor full of cards would entertain Maggie for a while. I played solitaire on my phone. One eye on the phone, one on the baby. At night, I played poker. But during the day, when I was watching Maggie, I wanted to keep it innocent.

After the settlement was finalized at the courthouse, I followed Verne home, his fucking Prius still on the road. He obeyed the speed limits. Turns out he lived five blocks from us, in an ash-and peach-colored mid-century modern house with a Christmas tree still up. It was May. Let's chalk that up to depression. But his grass was mowed and he set out his trash bins on the appropriate day. I considered that living.

Every day since then, I strapped Maggie into her stroller or into one of those baby-wearing carriers and we went for a walk. Back and forth past the mid-century house. I saw Verne in the window. He pretended he didn't see me and worked on his computer or played the piano. Even from the street, I could hear it was out of tune. He never drew the curtains closed.

I opened the box of cards and let the deck spill out. Most of the cards hit the ground in a pile and then scattered upon impact, but a few errant kings and queens and aces spiraled in the air before settling face-up on the floor. Maggie giggled and

busied herself with the cards. I resumed solitaire. We were playing cards together, I thought. Dr. Braunigan would approve of
this. *You must play with the girl*, he said at our last meeting. I
began seeing the therapist after Natalie's death. We go weekly.
I bring Maggie, eat a sandwich, and drink watery coffee in his
loft-like office overlooking a park. I give her one of those fruity
vegetable pouches. Sometimes two. We lunch together.

I did not tell Dr. Braunigan about our walks past Verne's
house. I also may have left out that I knew where Verne lived at
all. Certainly, Dr. Braunigan would say that it was my way of
circumventing the issues. I wouldn't disagree.

This morning I received a package in the mail. Inside were
our Christmas cards, designed by Natalie and ordered well in
advance of the holiday. Unfortunately, the box had gotten lost.
The company replaced them within days, but the initial box
never came. Long after the holiday and months after Natalie
died, in a mangled box, they arrived. I opened the package.
Wrapped in crisp white tissue were one hundred fifteen of them.
Love, Peace, and Happiness to You and Yours in the Upcoming Year!
Love, Natalie, Dan, and Maggie. A photo of our family amid fall
leaves at a local park. We'd hired a professional photographer for
the shoot. That's how Natalie referred to it: *Oh no, we can't meet
up that day, we have our photo shoot* or *What should we wear for
the shoot?* She wanted to be coordinated. I really didn't care and
thought the whole suburban tradition was stupid. In the end, we
all wore plaid. I considered our tartan family, looking straight
out of a catalog: *Get your plaid shirts and cable-knit sweaters and
happiness here—now with free shipping!* But we looked whole,
happy—I could admit that now. It was the kind of thing Natalie
thought about. Holiday cards and vaccinations and babysitters
and paying the cable bill.

I took out a few of the holiday cards. Natalie's smile was as bright as the sun's glare, artistically situated, and probably digitally enhanced, above us. If I received the card in the mail I'd have thought: *This. This is a genuinely happy family. I would like to be a part of it.* I took out another card. I brought it closer to my face. In my middle age, I had grown nearsighted. Maybe if I looked closer I'd catch a glimpse of what happened. Some hint. Surely it was there, right? I didn't see anything. I pulled out another card. Checked that one. Nothing. And another card, brought it to my eye, and still nothing. I was sure I was missing something. I pulled out another card. In the process, the thick ivory paper drew blood. I sucked the paper cut and turned the card. Maybe if I just looked at it at a certain angle. Another card. Tossed it aside with the rest of them. How can there be no evidence? The image was so believable.

I gathered Maggie up for an earlier walk than usual; we were making a special delivery. Up the hill we hiked. Though she was a bit old for it, I wore Maggie in the carrier, facing inward, since she was tired. She protested, but facing in, she was more likely to fall asleep. Two houses down, she was out. Her sweet snores warmed my chest where my shirt button was open. Outside the house, I slipped one of the holiday cards in his mailbox. I had written *Verne* in a loopy cursive with an evergreen gel pen. It was the pen Natalie had hoped to use to address the other cards. *I found the perfect pen*, she had said. I remembered that now, thinking how stupidly excited she was about a damned pen. I could see Verne at his piano. He wasn't playing, just staring at the keys. I didn't stand there long. I had done what I had come to do.

Now, having taken our daily walk earlier than usual, the day was dragging, which is why I resorted to the deck of cards as entertainment. Maggie sorted through the cards in a mysterious to me but clear to a toddler way. She was making piles. Holding up a card, making a determination, and putting it in one of three messy stacks. Outside, it began to rain. Water sluiced the air and pinged the thin bay window. We were always cold in that house. I watched the rhythmic assault of the rain and then I saw him. I hadn't seen him approach. Verne just appeared, standing across the street, situated squarely in the center of the window. He wore an olive green windbreaker with the hood up, looking not unlike a grim reaper. Indeed, that was who he was.

I dropped my phone and startled Maggie, who then noticed me noticing death in the window.

"Just a minute, sweetie," I said and scrambled to the front door.

"What the fuck? Get out of here," I yelled into the street. He didn't move. The rain came down heavier. Standing in the doorway, I was soaking through. I closed the glassed-in screen door and watched him.

A garbage truck thrummed by. A vibrant green cutting through the gray wet world. Strange for such a bright color to represent what we throw away, the things we want out of our lives. The truck stopped, a man in a Day-Glo vest hopped out and quickly dealt with my trash bins. When he climbed back in the truck and drove off, Verne was gone.

Maggie toddled up to my knee, pulling my pants leg. "Dada up. Dada. Up Dada. Dada. Mama. Dada, up?"

Later that night, on the news, I learned that Verne had jumped off a busy local bridge. The reporter stood in the blustery crosswinds and explained what happened, the best he could piece together. It happened after noon. A few passengers got out of their cars when they saw the man dive, but most cars kept driving, not wanting to stop their lives for his. *I know it's weird to say, but it was almost graceful*, a witness was telling the reporter.

Behind the two men, Verne's green jacket was tied to a balustrade, arms flapping in the wind. The reporter didn't know it belonged to the victim. *A tragedy*, the reporter said. His face was stoic but there was a rabid excitement in his eyes.

I wasn't sure what to do the next day. Did we go on our walk? Would it matter? I decided we still had to go out. Maggie needed the routine. I needed the routine. I pulled two tiny socks from her drawer. They didn't match, but I didn't think she would care. Natalie would have cared, but I didn't care. Should I care?

I installed Maggie, wrapped in a puffy jacket, into the stroller. She mimed that she wanted food. I'd prepared a snack cup of Goldfish, not the swimming, slimy kind, the find-in-your-car-and-in-your-pockets-and-in-your-couch kind. We trucked up the hill; this had been the extent of my exercise since Natalie died. I used to *hit the gym*. Isn't it funny, that term? I actually said it, too. *I'm going to hit the gym*, I'd say as Natalie cooked dinner and wore Maggie on her in a papoose. Baby-wearing, she called it. It seemed charming. Very village-like. I liked it—multitasking. I'd hit the gym and shower in the luxury shower provided and then come home an hour later to the savory smells of whatever Natalie had cooked. The baby was already asleep. Natalie and I ate together while she asked about my day. I sometimes asked about hers. *Mom group and crying and ohmygod and chapped nipples and the park*. But the specifics were hazy. Fuck. I can barely throw nuggets in the oven or open one of those pouches for Maggie without losing it. Natalie really was amazing. Wife. Mom. Person. All those things. I bet she made a stellar ghost.

I took Maggie to the park. She pointed at the swings, those black rubber seats with holes for their tiny legs. I pushed her but didn't look at her. I looked behind her. I looked at her feet. I couldn't look at her. Right now, it was just us. That asshole, that dead asshole, had taken a piece of our story with him over the bridge. I was glad he was gone, but concerned that he and Natalie might be in the same place. I didn't believe in heaven and hell and all that. But if Verne even shared the same soil, well, I couldn't even think about that. Maggie laughed and I looked to see what it was. A crow had stolen her snack cup. "Shoo! Get away," I yelled. The crow flew off and took the cup with it. I couldn't even feed the child.

The high school students from the neighboring school approached. First one, then three, then many. They climbed the playground equipment, far too small for their adult-sized bodies. They ate their lunches, yelled at each other, laughed, and displayed an array of love—puppy-sweet and scary-real. The school bell rang and the kids scurried back, leaving behind greasy lunch trays and empty milk pints. The whole time I pushed Maggie. It wasn't a very long lunch break. They had, mercifully, left a wide berth for us, keeping our experiences separate. I appreciated that.

The news was still covering the jump. For a few days, the jumper was anonymous. There hadn't been a jump at that bridge in eight years. Flowers were collected and a teddy bear had been tied to a pole; the string had come loose, causing the bear to dangle. The anonymous jumper's body hit some crags below that had beaten his body so terrifically, the only thing left was a pulpy carcass. The reporters said it in a more diplomatic way, but that was the gist. He wasn't recognizable. No one had phoned in a missing person in the vicinity. No one missed the guy.

The next day, we walked to the house. The curtains were drawn. I waited a while. Maggie stirred in the stroller. "Up Dada. Up Dada. Go." I saw nothing move, so we turned around and went home.

A while later, a sign for an estate sale went up. With Maggie at a neighbor's, I dared to go in. Two ladies clearly unrelated to the deceased sat at a makeshift register. A third woman ushered me in.

"Hi," she chirped. "Just make an offer."

"Thanks," I mumbled, and felt the cash in my pocket. I didn't come to buy, but felt that if I had cash with me, it'd be more believable. Otherwise, they might toss me out. Interloper! Murderer, they could say. But they didn't.

Though clean, the house was showing its wear. Trim pulled away from the walls. Wood paneling was beginning to warp at corners. Orange and brown throw blankets covered the couch—dated, but handmade. The piano sat where I knew it would be, the whites yellowing, an ebony key missing. On the mantel, a pewter and brass picture frame showed a woman. A girl, really. The styling of the photo indicated it was from the 1970s. I recognized Verne, probably in his early twenties. In the photo, his hands encircled the girl's waist. The photo was in soft focus, little haloes emanating from their bodies; they seemed happy. Another snap on a beach, he was backlit and he held his hand aloft, saluting the photographer.

Old Christmas ornaments; a Radio Flyer wagon; a vintage sled; piles and piles of books on religion, many of them: Buddhism, Gnosticism, Christianity, Islam, Judaism. Corningware and Pyrex and enamel Scandinavian things piled high on the kitchen counters. They were the belongings of a man who had lived in the house a long time.

A calendar from the local tire place hung on the refrigerator. I flipped back a few months to the date. I was hoping to see something. I don't know what. What would Verne have written? *Day I turned into a murderer?* The fourth—there was something written there. Between *Alex bdy* and a Thursday with nothing going on was a barely legible notation. *4:00 Mona.* Nothing more. Four o'clock. Natalie was killed at 3:56. Well, she was declared dead at 3:56. She had been lying there for a while before her crushed body was spatulaed up and taken away.

I wondered about Mona. Was she the woman in the photos? Was she who Verne claimed to be going to the airport for? What would have happened if she'd had to wait? I ran my finger along the top of a nearby shelf. It came away covered in dust, the ash of life. I rubbed it away on my pants leg. I went down a hallway, the tread of my boots feeling wrong on the blushing thick carpet. There were so many doors, but only one was open. At the end of the hallway was the master bedroom. I entered. This was the room where the man who killed my wife once slept. Were Verne's nights filled with horrors? Guilt? Love? Hope? Were they filled with my Nat?

There was an en-suite bathroom. Small, of course—standard for the time period. Pink and black tiling. On the sink counter was a worn bar of soap. Irish Spring, it had been. I could still make out the *I* and the *ng.* I thought about the path his hands had to take to wear down the bar in such a way. Did he wring his hands? Did he scrub so hard to get rid of the filth? A toilet paper roll nearing its end with only tatters of paper hanging on waited by the toilet.

I heard someone else enter the bedroom and I quickly abandoned the room. There was nothing for sale in there. I hurried back down the hall. The stale pink of the place was stifling. It was forty-year-old air. I needed to get out. But then I saw her. It was the woman in the photos. She was much older, of course, but the hairstyle was the same: wavy bangs with a tight, short ponytail. Grayer, naturally. The skin more worn, less elastic. She was standing in front of the mantel, looking at the past. She didn't touch anything. Her hands were tucked into the pockets of her skirt. Was this Mona? I wondered. I wanted to ask. I wiped my upper lip, where sweat had beaded, and walked into the living room. What would I say? She turned, suddenly, and I picked up a tchotchke from a nearby table, feigning innocent interest.

"They call it a Kokopelli," she said. She had a lilt that I hadn't expected—Irish? Scottish? "It's a Hopi fertility deity," she told me.

"Yeah, I know. I—" Why was I nervous? "I've been to Scottsdale." I turned the figure over in my hand.

"Lovely place. But have you been to Sedona?" she asked. It was all very amiable. What did she know of the man Verne had become? What did I know of the man Verne was?

"No, just Scottsdale," I said.

"With your wife?" she asked, nodding to my wedding ring. That was where the card deck had come from. Scottsdale. A babymoon, Natalie had called it. She pregnant as hell, me trying my best to keep up with her cravings for Dr. Pepper and quesadillas. The Kokopelli, bands of them playing their little flutes at the gift shop and framed on our hotel room wall. She said something about how they were our guiding spirits, taking us into parenthood through the sluicing rain of a desert storm.

"Yeah. My wife," I said. I wanted to ask her if she remembered when Verne got the little figurine. Was she with him? Are you Mona? I wanted to ask. Are you the reason Verne was late and killed my wife and left me spiritually amputated and unable to breathe? I wanted to ask these things. I wanted to strangle this sweet woman who wore pastels and an outdated hairstyle. She seemed kind. I wanted her dead. I studied the fringe of the rug beneath me. I felt bile in my throat. I fingered the sharp edges of the Kokopelli in my hand.

"Are you Mona? I spit out. But she had already walked past me. I could see her backside out the front window. She walked out of my view. She was gone. I bought the Kokopelli with the few dollars I had. I didn't negotiate; I paid the price as marked.

When You Shower in Your Clothes

When you shower in your clothes, you feel the weight on your shoulders. And on your hips. And on your thighs. And on your ankles. When you shower in your clothes, you wonder why you never did it before. You wonder why you are doing it now. You think about where you are going to dry your heavy, wet, sinking clothing. You don't want to flood the room and you don't have any hanging racks.

When you shower in your clothes you do it because you are unprepared to greet your body after the inevitable betrayal. All the loofah in the sea cannot slough off that which has been left on you like an oil slick, slowly killing everything in its wake.

Your oversized sweater and long Hawaiian-print skirt float on the surface of the water. When you vomit, it tastes like that battery you licked when you were ten. Even the word *battery* evokes metal and salt on your tongue.

When you shower in your clothes, you don't turn on the light. By nightlight and moonlight through the window, you see all you need to. The nightlight was a gift from your mother after she moved to Fort Lauderdale. Its shiny seashell emits a pink light and looks not unlike a woman's private parts. You told your mother this when she gave it to you. She frowned and said good girls don't think like that. It was a tiger cowrie shell; you looked it up. They are native to the waters of Africa and Polynesia, not to south Florida.

Beneath the nightlight is the scale your mother gave you when you moved into your apartment. *Happy 20s! Now go have fun!* the notecard read. You weighed yourself on it before you left tonight. You wonder if you weigh less or more now.

When you sit on the bathtub floor in your clothes that feel like quicksand, you hear your neighbors clanking dishes on the other side of the wall. You hear the baby crying. The baby always cries, but that means it's alive, right?

With your numb fingers you pick at the sides of the mat that is suctioned to the bottom of the bathtub. You pull up a corner and hear the *pop, pop, suck* as it disengages with the porcelain tub. Underneath are circles of pink, mildew or mold. You are bathing in a petri dish. The mat is meant to keep you from slipping and still you are slipping anyway. You may fall and become so small you'll slide down the water trail into the drain and into the pipes and into the walls and then who would let you out and would you be trapped there? One of those haunted faces on the other side of the wall with no features, but familiar enough to still pass as somewhat human.

While you imagine drowning in the shower you wince at the way the bar of soap abrades your skin. It hurts, this skin of yours. Torn and stretched and poisoned. Every drop of water a dagger, every lavender soap bubble noxious. You could spend hours at those bath-and-body places, where the walls are lined with multicolored, multi-scented potions. Cherry Blossom

Bouquet, Pineapple Breeze, Peppermint Punch; they all sound like cocktail names at a mock-Polynesian bar.

You don't take off your clothes because underneath is your body and you cannot imagine looking at your body as you once did. As your own.

When the water cools, you think, *This is penance.* The pores of your skin pucker to tiny sharp tips. Protection, but where was this armor when you needed it earlier? Earlier you were like bread, soft and easy to cut. No, not cut, rip.

You shiver. You think: *I will freeze it out and off of me.* Your hair hangs limply, strands sticking to your cheek and your forehead. The heat is completely gone now. You slam your fist against the knob. Instead of turning the water off, it switches to the lower faucet and the tub begins to fill. Your skirt drifts away from your body and creates a drain cover. You let this happen and feel the glacial waters seep over and through your clothes and your skin and your blood and your muscles. When the bathtub fills halfway, it submerges your knees and your hips and your ass that he said was *niiiiiiice* before he came and before he pushed you aside and said *all done.* You turn the water off. Is this what a baptism feels like?

You lie down in the water. Push your body into the cold, your chest into the tub's bottom. You put your head forward and down. Hold your breath. *One. Two. Three. Four.* Your hair floats in a halo. You are like Medusa. *Five. Six. Seven.* You get to thirty-four and come up for air, a whale breaching. You want to slap your own body down into the water and feel the pain, but you're not as graceful as a whale.

When you shower in your clothes, you realize there are corners and crevices of your body that are inaccessible, for you alone to reach. You peel off your clothes. Survey your prickled skin.

You eventually throw your clothes directly in the trash. You put on new clothes, something never worn before. Drain the tub. Pull up the bathmat and scrub the tiny filthy suction cups. Inhale the cleansing bleach smell. See the stars, or pretend to, above the city's own aurora. Open the window and leave the room.

The Space Where They Meet

When I'm not avoiding the cafeteria at lunchtime, I'm in the far stall of the girls' second-floor bathroom making diagrams and graphs and pie charts. My favorite are Venn diagrams. You know, the ones where there are two (sometimes more) circles and they cross over for a certain amount of space and that space means *something important?*

Intangible things—things like feelings and hope—meet the tangible circles in a Venn diagram, and in that overlap is where the answers to my questions are; I'm sure of it. I like making Venns. Trying to figure out answers.

Things like the number of times I cheated on a test vs. number of times I was cheated off of; maybe they cancel each other out. Girls in school who say they like Christina Aguilera and girls in school who say they like Britney. I made a third circle, too, for Destiny's Child, and that circle only overlapped with the others the tiniest amount. The girls in school who don't know I exist vs. those who just know my name vs. *yeah, I've seen you around.* The middle of that one was "me, maybe not invisible." Etc., etc., etc.

The soap in the school bathrooms is this powdery stuff, and you have to push up on this metal contraption to get it out. I've never seen it anywhere but in a school. I tasted it once—Leanne Powers and her posse said I dissed her mom and so made me eat the soap. I didn't diss her mother. I just said, "Yeah, your mom," which I'd heard on *SNL* and from kids in school. I was just trying it out. The soap was gritty on my tongue but dissolved quickly, leaving behind the taste of roses and rubbing alcohol. It's good, I told Leanne and Brianne and Rebecca. And then I took more into my palm, push, push, push, and licked it real slow. *Gross*, they said and walked out. I counted to ten before I threw up.

That was the first day of the school year and I knew it wasn't going to get better from there.

But after that Tuesday, they left me alone. I often caught them looking over their shoulders and pointing at me. I made more Venn diagrams in the weeks that followed. Kids who had parents killed in the Twin Towers vs. parents that escaped. Parents that were gone vs. those that exist in some real way; that was an interesting one since I hadn't defined what "gone" meant.

I moved in with my father; my parents had been divorced since I was three. My father lived outside the school district lines by .48 miles. They set it up so I'd stay in the same school. They told me I was lucky.

Under the stained-glass light that hung above the kitchen table, I marched my socked feet on the sticky floor so I could hear the sssssssssssssuccccck of the ghost of something sticky. I sat at that table until late in the night, long after my dad came home from his job at Lowe's. And into the night I diagrammed: amount of paper that could fly out a window vs. float vs. paper used by the printer everyone gets to use in the school library. Missing person signs with smiling faces vs. not smiling faces and the space in the intersection was missing persons in front of Christmas trees.

I kind of know these intersections don't mean anything. They aren't measuring anything.

A big one: the time it takes for a man to fall one hundred stories vs. the time it takes to sharpen a pencil. In that intersection I wrote: *the time it took for me to understand.* So, you see, it didn't take long for the paper in front of me to explain things. No wings ever appeared and the pencil was so sharp; I pushed it against the soft skin of my neck until I felt the tiny puncture and all the air go out of me. The wound was so small you wouldn't even know it was there.

I used to use a protractor but realized there was quite a margin for error with the circles, so I got a compass. One of those metal things that holds a pencil and has a really sharp point you place in the middle. You turn, turn, turn, and the pencil makes a perfect circle. A compass punctures skin faster than a sharpened No. 2 pencil, you should know. A compass can be so many things. Also: a navigational compass, a moral compass. Maybe my mom needed a compass to see which way was up.

Circles are so perfect. You can predict what will happen in a circle. Radius, circumference: a pie a moon a sun a face the iris of an eye a wheel an orange the turbine engine of a plane.

My diagrams are where geometry and life meet and I don't care if I'm doing them right or not. Anyway, that's what I tell my teacher when she finds one mistakenly stuck to a ditto I turn in for homework. She just smiles all lopsided, hands it back with my C+ essay about *The Tempest* and says, "Nice work." She puts her hand on my shoulder and I think her eyes tear up a little, but it's hard to tell because she wears these thick wide-rimmed glasses. The diagram that got stuck was this one:

Circling

"You just have to turn it a little," Deirdre is saying. I have a wire hanger dug deep into some muck in the bathroom sink.

"We should've used Drano," I say, tugging the wire toward me. It seems to be stuck.

"That stuff'll kill you. Poison."

"But it works," I point out. "This isn't working."

"If you can get the angle right, you can just . . ." and something comes loose, sending me backward into the shower door. I'm on the floor with a mildewy towel on my head, still wet from the previous night's shower. The wire is beside me and at the end of it is a goldfish, mouth still gasping for air. The fish's mouth keeps working the oxygen, not even noticing that its guts are pouring out of it like a cream sauce, where the wire stabbed.

"Uh," I say. Except she is unfolding another hanger. One eye closed, she peers down the drain like it's a periscope.

"I don't think that was the problem," she says.

"Of course that was the problem. There was a fish in our drain!"

"No, no, I think I see something else." She stuffs the wire down. "I think I might . . ." And then I notice the fish has stopped moving.

"It's dead," I say. She doesn't turn around. With the towel in my hand I grab the tail and toss it into the small wicker wastebasket; a trail of creamed guts is laid out on the floor. Deirdre pops her lips, like she herself is a fish.

All triumph and strength, she works her way down the wire and tugs. "Got it!" she cries. First, one small leg is waving about; tiny suction cups line the appendage. It's an octopus. A very tiny golden octopus. It is the same color as Deirdre's wedding ring and a couple of its legs are wrapped around the wire.

"Well, aren't you cute," she says, practically tickling its chin with her sing-song voice.

"Deirdre, this is weird shit," I say. Because it is.

The sink had been backing up for nearly a month. Tendrils of toothpaste would swim around the surface of the dirty sink water before it disappeared down the drain, leaving a ring of dirt around the bowl of the sink, occasional turquoise flourishes. It didn't bother me, but a month ago, on one surprising and hasty visit to the room for sex, Deirdre pronounced it disgusting and said "that needs to be fixed."

The guest bedroom and corresponding bathroom became my own after recurring episodes of banishment from our bed. I didn't mind the plastic shower. I didn't mind the Laura Ashley floral decor. Deirdre and I had been having issues. We had to talk. We both spat it occasionally: *We have to talk.* But we kept getting too busy, too preoccupied, too complacent. Maybe we were just hopeful.

Finally, on Halloween night, after she chastised the last trick-or-treater on how sugar would destroy them, I decided then.

I said, "Deidre, we have to talk." She sighed her annoying asthmatic sigh and motioned me to follow her into the guest bathroom. I ran ahead of her and said "Let me just—" and I beat her to the tiny room, where I had left the remnants of twelve mini Twix bars. The room had become my private sanctuary in which to commit heinous crimes of gluttony and self-service. Or, she would deem it so. I stuffed the wrappers into my shorts and flushed the toilet. I made a pass at my hands under the cold tap. Even that small amount of water pooled there for a moment, a cesspool, before finally draining.

"I didn't hear you close the toilet seat," she quipped, and I turned to check my mistake. Surely I'd be busted. It was down.

"I did it quietly." Ignoring me, she pushed me aside.

"Might as well get some of the stuff around the house done," she muttered. "I'll just have to do it myself." But as I grabbed the heavy red bottle of Drano, she said there was a better way.

Several wire hangers later, we are no closer to marital bliss or an unclogged drain. She lifts the toilet seat lid and places the octopus in the bowl.

"A little water for now," she says. The octopus stares back at me, minuscule knowing eyeballs on its head. "Then we can figure out what to do with it. Now, let's test it out." She runs the faucet. First hot, then cold, until the sink fills. It is clear that it is still clogged.

"We should call a professional," I say, rising to stand beside Deirdre, wishing I could put my arm around her waist. It is a beautiful waist. When pregnant, she worried about the loss of her hourglass. But the sands never filled successfully and we never had children. After the third try, she had grown bitter then sad then bitter again, and here we are. I think she is getting back to sad.

"No, I can manage it," Deirdre says. She gets down on her back under the sink. She shoves aside the extra toilet paper, hair dryer, and a stack of vintage *Playboys*. She is working a wrench at the pipes. I didn't know she knew what a wrench even was. I had loved that about her, actually. Just when you underestimated her, thinking she was a cheerleader sorority type, she could lift a couple hundred pounds or she would quote Keats or Shakespeare or something she read in *The New Yorker*.

"Maybe you shouldn't be right under it," I say.

"Do you want to just do it then?" No. I didn't really want to do it.

"I told you I think we should call a pro—"

"We aren't calling anyone. This is our issue. Our thing. We'll figure it out." But I notice she moves her body aside, just a little. She finally jimmies something free and the pipe opens up in her hands.

"A squid? A goddamn squid. What the fuck?" I call out.

"I think it might be a cuttlefish," she says, "it's cute." She cups the creature in her hands and then sets it in the toilet to join the octopus, who is slowly climbing the walls of the bowl. Periodically, I see a little crimson leg waving over the side. It's changed color. The air is growing salty. The stink of low tide is settling in. The climbing vines on the wallpaper are beginning to look more like seaweed and I feel like I'm slowly drowning.

"Does this not seem weird to you?" I ask her.

"What?"

"What? The fish, the dead goldfish. The fish in the toilet. In the toilet! We have fish in our toilet!"

"They're cephalopods, Andy." Deirdre had once wanted to be a marine biologist, she'll tell anyone who'll listen. But that was long ago, and the most training she'd had were a few class trips to the aquarium.

"Wait, there's something else," Deirdre says, and I see her hand disappear into the pipe. The *Playboys* are getting wet. Very wet, and I lunge toward the pile to save them. We used to look at them together, Deirdre and I. We'd laugh about Goldie Hawn perched in a gigantic martini glass and the absurd sexual styles of the '70s, but then kiss and it'd all be lush and incredible from there. Afterward, we would drink ice water and turn on the white string lights in our bedroom. Brunch in the morning. Always. Depending on if it was a weekday or not, breakfast or brunch out after sex. French toast and pancakes and the salty crisp of bacon between our lips while we played a volatile game of footsie under the table.

She yanks and I see a purple thick finger emerge. First one, then another. It's a starfish. A fucking starfish. WhatthehellwasgoingonandwhywasthePacificemptyingintomysink!?

"Starfish!" I exclaim.

"Sea star," she corrects.

"I know that. Did you know"—here I wanted her to see I wasn't a complete moron—"I hear there's some sort of starfish disease going around and they're all turning into sludge." She only looks at me. Dead eyes. Like the goldfish. Except with lashes. Long lashes that collect snow and tears in equal measure, and with the wetness, it always looks like she is wearing mascara these days.

Right then, I know it's not my fault. Or hers. I know that I still love her and maybe she still loves me. But after all the strokes we made toward each other day after day, we got tired, and now we're just barely treading water.

"Well. This one seems okay," I say. I smile. I don't know why. It seems the right thing to do. When she finally gets the body out of the pipe, we can see it's injured. One of its legs is just hanging off. It's hard to tell if it is in pain, though I imagine it is. The star is resting in the palm of Deirdre's hand. With a face turned away, how can you tell if it's in pain?

"Hang on, little buddy," I say to the mottled purple star. It seems to tense and becomes a more crumpled version of itself.

"Here, take it," Deirdre says, as she pushes it my way. I do not want to touch the thing. Who knows where it came from and, anyway, it was in our plumbing, which I know has got to be filled with dirty seething things. I back away.

"Andy. Take it. Just take it. It's hurt. I'll be right back."

I don't want to. I want to absolve myself from any responsibility. I look at Deirdre. The false mascara is caking. She is about to lose it. She presses the thing into my arms and runs from the room.

I am holding a starfish. A sea star. Whatever.

"Are you hurting?" I ask it. I pet it with one finger. Its craggy skin is tough and so brightly purple I think it has to be a reaction to some chemical we humans have inserted into its habitat. It is harshly beautiful. I want to turn it over. See its face. I flip it, but in doing so, it slips, slimy from the drain residue. I catch it by its injured leg, but then drop it again. It splats on the linoleum. There are a few lesions on the underbelly, I can see. I think it's already dead. I think it was dead when we pulled it from the drain.

I look at the goldfish in its wicker wastebasket grave. At the toilet aquarium we've created. I hear Deirdre returning. I slip my hand underneath the star. I hold it close. I whisper to it. Deirdre has a large plastic container with water. We usually use it for soup. I gently put the sea star in its new tank. I don't tell her I think it is dead.

The Balloon Animal Artist
Goes to a Funeral

The balloon animal artist had worked some weird gigs before, so
when he showed up at Langley Brothers Funeral Home, he was a
little thrown off, but thought, well this was the life of a balloon animal artist. As soon as he set foot inside the heavy, ornately carved
door, he knew he should've dressed for the occasion. Instead, he
had thought of it as a gig, so he wore his mustard corduroys and tie-
dye T-shirt. Stupid, he thought. His mother would be comically, but
painfully, hitting him over his head, if she knew. If she were alive.

"Oh, you must be Jack," a heavy-set woman said. She was
about his mother's age and wore an appropriate charcoal skirt
suit. She shook his hand and told him to follow her. The air in the
building was yellow—the walls beige, a riot of paisley carpet. It
smelled like dried flowers and the potent perfume of the woman,
who had not yet introduced herself.

"You can be here," she said, and held up her two hands in what
seemed like surrender, but he knew her hands were saying, stay

here. Stay. She continued to hold her hands up and Jack studied them—if he was into palm reading and all that, he'd say she would have a long and busy life. That she'd be rich, that she'd find love—all based on the map of indentations running on her palms. He finally nodded, and she walked off.

There were at least a hundred people in the room. Some sat on the flimsy folding chairs, some talked in murmured voices. Beyond them was the casket. FREDERICK ARMEE read the sash attached to a spray of purple and red flowers. The casket was cracked open, but Jack couldn't see anything other than a hint of white satin sheen. There was a dead body in there, he knew, but thinking about it took the air from his chest, so he set about work.

Out of his apron, he pulled a thin red balloon. He'd start with a dog—simple, classic.

The only funeral he'd been to was his mother's two years before. She raised him in a one-bedroom house—marketed as a "cottage." The linoleum peeled and faint lines of mildew ran up the walls. She worked as a waitress at one of those 1950s-style diners off the interstate. All chrome and a cacophony of oldies issuing from miniature jukeboxes at each table.

When he'd get suspended from school, he spent long fried-egg-and-milkshake days with her at work and left knowing the words to almost every Elvis song and smelling like smoky meat. *Pansy*, his mother called him. *Go fucking shower.* He didn't tell her that she, too, always smelled like that. He didn't say, maybe that's why no one loves you.

Jack blew into the latex balloon, felt the air leave his lungs for the benefit of his craft. He tied a quick knot, twisted and turned the oblong thing, twisted and turned. The latex squeaked in the hush of the room. When he was done, he perched the dog on his palm, waiting to give it to someone. But people just stared at him. He placed the little dog on the table beside him and started working on something else. Out came a green balloon—longer; he'd make a dragon. Out goes the air. Alive goes his creature. He worked quickly.

He had made several animals and two swords before the woman approached him again, this time with a young man in tow. Tall, very tall—though Jack himself was six two—and dressed in a black suit with a purple silky shirt beneath. He was probably a year or two younger than Jack.

"THIS is Jack," the woman said.

"This IS Jack," the tall man repeated.

"This is JACK," the woman said again. It was like one of those drama exercises used to show how different intonations held different meanings.

"Can I ask you a question?" The man didn't wait for Jack to reply. "Did you know your father?"

"No," Jack said. Slowly, slowly, the balloon he held in his hand released air. He felt it deflate in his palm.

"Where is your mother these days?" the woman asked. He wondered at the question. This woman knew his mother. Had known. Once.

"She died." Beat. Beat. The silence between them only lasted a couple seconds, but Jack could swear he heard the air leave the room.

"Right, I remember her, that Margie. Spitfire, that one. I had to wrestle my Fred away." Her eyes grew big and bright—an old-school camera flash. "No offense," she said. Jack blinked. "I remember one time when—"

Jack stopped listening and walked away into the crush of mourners. Starchy black fabrics brushed his skin as people milled around him, several heads turning in his direction, following his movements. The face in the casket had the same narrow pointed nose, spidery long lashes as Jack. He waited for a yearning, something in his sternum, but nothing came.

Jack resumed his position in the corner. A child, wandering by, seemed interested, so Jack fashioned him a quick yellow giraffe. The boy squealed and ran off, presumably to show his parents. Only Jack knew that later, the animal would expire. First the leg—maybe it'd be a prick by an unassuming zipper, or maybe with time or cold air, the balloon would begin to wither. Then the torso, then the rest of the appendages. The kid would be left with a shriveled handful of latex and a sheen of ashy powder on his hands.

The Best Thing for the Baby

After I lost the baby, I kept going to the prenatal yoga classes. I had bought a ten-class card and had only used four. It'd be such a waste to not use them. At the end of class, we lay in savasana after being told by Lotus, the teacher, that we are doing the best thing for the baby. That *I* am doing the best thing for *my* baby. That I am being present in such an important time in my baby's creation.

I still have a belly pooch. *The swelling will go down*, they said. *In time*, they said. But it's been a month and every time I chant *oooommmmm* I feel the vibrations in my uterus. Maybe because it is hollow now; I don't know. I sometimes still feel her kicks.

I got an email the other day about how, after my baby is born, I still have three months to get things off my registry for 10 percent off. I deleted the email. I should just delete the registry altogether; this morning I got a message saying that my cousin purchased us the baby cot. We haven't gotten around to telling everyone.

Actually, we haven't gotten around to telling anyone.

After class I'm in my Volvo, purchased for maximum baby safety. It's a bit too large and reminds me of a station wagon. For now, Doug and I fill the space with uncomfortable silence. But the extra trunk space is nice.

I think I'd make a terrible mother; I didn't even know when I lost her. I went in for my regular appointment and oh, the stillness that filled the air, like a muted electricity. The doctor was mid-sentence when the hush took over. It wasn't a monumental silence. I could still hear honking cars outside, four stories down. An alert being sounded over the PA out in the hospital corridor. My breathing. But I didn't hear the *thwomp-thwomp-thwomp*. No one did. The hush was reserved for the room we were in, a cocoon; it held us in its embrace. Maybe if we said nothing, it would be fine. The heart would be found—small, beating, hopeful—and everyone would collectively breathe again, smile and say, *There it is! Sneaky little dodger, that one!*

That didn't happen. And when the door pushed open, the hush exhaled right out of the room and in came a maelstrom of medical jargon and *you're being sent down to imaging for an ultrasound.* They didn't even ask. Off we went, Doug and I and our dead fetus, though we didn't know it at the time. She was still the size of an eggplant and still had a name, Bella.

The technician was kind. She ensured I was warm, covered me with blankets taken out of some sort of heating unit. She moved slowly, deliberately. A doctor I did not know was also in the room. He watched, arms crossed, teeth pulling at one corner of his lip. He stood in the corner, there to make the pronouncement. When he did, he uncrossed his arms, whispered something to the technician, put his thick hand on Doug's shoulder. *I'm sorry.*

I really liked that technician. She was a twenty-something girl with a bouncy blond ponytail and an effervescent way about her. She wasn't bubbly in a daft sort of way, she just seemed to really enjoy her job. On a previous visit, she'd shared that she, too, wanted children and *Oh! A girl!* It was like she was as happy for me as she would be for herself.

She cried. I don't remember her name. But when I started heaving and Doug wiped a tear from his face, her eyes watered up, too. Then she excused herself, and for a short while before I was taken away for the procedure, Doug and I sat by ourselves in the purple glow in a room made up of plastics and rubber and rustling paper sheets. But the warm blankets helped.

At the beginning of yoga class, we go around sharing our names, how far along we are, and if we're experiencing any pain or have any issues we would like addressed.

Elaine. 27 weeks. The pain is immeasurable.

Handprints

You are so beautiful, they say. Please. Don't move. Not a muscle. Those lashes. Those eyes. I bet all the boys . . . This is why they say the Order took Louise in. Her beauty. They usually only took in the boys.

Louise doesn't hear their words. It is unclear to the men of the Order if she even can.

She hasn't spoken since they took her in. But her hands, her hands are perfection, they whisper to each other. They don't want anyone else to claim her apricot palm, her delicate fingers.

Please. Put your hand here. They direct her to a large pan of dark paint. She places her hand down gently. They put their rough hands atop hers and push, push down on top. Her wrist bends slightly, aches, arches up. But they bear down again. When they release, she lifts her hand and studies the black dye. The lines and ridges of her skin. Love line. Life line, all darkened, yet somehow more visible. Her mother had told her about these roads in the skin, before.

Before her mother died—her own life line abridged, before Louise was taken in by these men. Before, when she thought she understood what her life line meant. Now, Louise tries to follow her life line but the men grab her hand again and press it against the wall. And again and again. They are making wallpaper with her handprints. Louise was here, it will say. She tries to high five herself but they will not permit this exaltation.

When Louise is long gone from the room, from the building, from the Order that would define and defy her, her life line is still a fractured branch. Her knuckles grow twisted and fat, earlier than they should have; she is still young. Nubs of ginger, her husband lovingly calls them. They hurt all the time.

Her branching love line will be the truest indicator of her life. She has children. She has a husband. Her husband dies. Her children grow up, have children of their own. She finds love again. She pats their heads, holds her grandchildren's cheeks for kisses. She sews Halloween costumes for them, frosts many cakes, and kneads dough for bread. Grasps their own tiny hands in hers to help cut with scissors. They love the rose scent of her hands and allow them to rest on their own skin a beat longer than many would.

When Louise is old, the Order is outed on television. Abuse, they say, of the little boys under the care of such rough and secretive men. The Order disbands. Some of the men are imprisoned. Some become schoolteachers. The boys in their care are sent elsewhere. The building they occupied is abandoned.

Louise starts talking about a place where she crawled the walls. Climbing, climbing, looking for an escape, a hatch, a ladder, the top of the well. Her grandchildren listen, rapt, to these tales of adventure. Her grown children think it is dementia. They talk to Louise in hushed tones primarily reserved for libraries and chapels and funeral homes.

Take these arthritic hands, she begs. They are folded like origami, hiding something.

A family buys the Order's abandoned property and turns it into a single-family home. We can just paint over it, says the six-months-pregnant woman, of the handprint wallpaper. No, no, her husband says. He picks at a corner and pulls. The wallpaper comes off easily. Tear rip tear.

So much work to do, he says. Strips of handprints come down and are tossed into the trash. Many miles away, Louise pulls at the skin on her hands, the eczema in the webs between her fingers on fire. A flare-up. The garbage truck will collect Louise's wallpaper hands.

Later, her ghost prints will climb mountains of junk, trash, non-biodegradables. Louise will die clasping her hands. *She is so beautiful*, the nurse thinks as he closes the old woman's eyes, something he's not supposed to do, but has seen done in the movies as a sign of respect. Louise's hands will roam the earth, a thumbprint on the bottom of someone's shoe, a piece of her pinkie on the snout of a stray dog, on the wind. Some handprints face down as if clutching the earth. Full palms lie open toward the heavens, her life line still intact. Her love line still living.

Maude's Cards and Humanity

Aaron Burr.

Maude has sex dreams of Aaron Burr. Except he looks like Steve Buscemi, but she knows it is actually Aaron Burr. They lie in bed together, with no shirts and very high thread count sheets up to their nipples, and debate things like tantric sex, single-origin coffee, and the GDP.

Spontaneous human combustion.

At the café, when the patron who comes in daily and orders a cup of hot water with lemon and two packets of sugar explodes, no one is sitting near him. Oh sure, bits of muscle and spatters of blood sully the clothing of the other customers, but there are no other fatalities or injuries. After the body (strands of it, chunks) is taken away, the café owner, Maude, decides the wall looks like art. She and her baristas are always trying to bring in local artists. Amateur watercolors of lakes and sunsets in Ikea frames never sell. Same with collages made from grocery receipts and dollar bills—some notion of anti-capitalism that never really sits well with Maude.

Maude types out index cards:

> *Study in TNT*
> *Café Luna Gallery*
> *Opening night, March 14, 2016*

People come after hours and want wine and beer, not tea and coffee, and Maude realizes she does not know what goes into a gallery's opening night. Artists are not the same. They expect more. But still, one man, in a beanie and a Members Only jacket, wishes to purchase the art.

"I'm afraid it's not for sale," Maude tells him.

"Nonsense," he says, dipping two fingers in his cappuccino and sucking the foam with his two front rabbit teeth. She thinks about it awhile and two days later, jackhammers and workmen procured from outside Home Depot remove a portion of the wall. The buyer comes in a pickup truck and it takes two men and four women to haul it into the truck bed. The café now has a gaping hole in its side and when people drive by, they'd say: *Oh hey, that's where that guy exploded.*

Old-people smell.

After work, most days, Maude travels the thirty-one miles to Whispering Hollow, the home for those with dementia where she'd stationed her mother the year before. Her mother, only sixty-four, shuffles through a pack of cards with the dexterity of a Vegas card shark while staring out the window. Regina, the nurse, kindly spoon-feeds her dinner while Maude eats tuna fish out of the can. *Lovely seeing you, Sarah,* her mother says when she leaves.

Finger painting.

Maude's pinky drifted through the green. *You're doing it wrong,* said her sister, Sarah, who, at six, knew how to manage such things as art.

Cuddling.

Aaron Burr/Steve Buscemi is morally opposed to cuddling.

Seppuku.

Sarah, Maude's sister, was a fan of old samurai films: *Zatoichi, Seven Samurai,* and the like. She even had an antique samurai sword hung on display over her fireplace. She was an intern at an art museum. One night, after the museum had closed, a doddering docent turned out to be not so doddering and raped her three times under the accusing scribbles of Jackson Pollock. Sarah returned to the Modern Hall Gallery a week later and gutted herself with the samurai sword. She had also set fire to the Pollock, and as her innards spilled, she reached for the painting, causing her fingers to blister. This they could tell from the autopsy. The volcanic blisters were what Maude remembered when she identified the body.

A defective condom.

Maude pretends Mark is Aaron Burr. It makes the whole thing bearable. She'd been trying to make it bearable for a year now.

My inner demons.

A young man with a delicate blond bun atop his head comes into the café with a large black portfolio under his arm. He asks to speak to the manager. Maude talks to him as he tells her of his craft and his calling. *My Inner Demons*, he says, is the name of the collection. He pulls out print after print of ill-conceived Georgia O'Keeffe reproductions.

Winking at old people.
She brings one of the not-O'Keeffes to her mother's that night. Tapes it up on the wall with masking tape. The following evening, Maude finds it under the bed with a photo of Maude when she was nine, wearing a leotard and tap shoes. Also under the bed: a misshapen paper clip, a penny from 1958, an empty cigar box, a VHS tape of a film called *Crimson Bat*, and three socks. Doesn't anyone clean the rooms in this place? When Maude leaves, she takes all of the under-bed findings with her. Two old men walk by her as she heads down the hallway. They both wink at her. She winks back.

Establishing dominance.
In the car, on the ride home, Maude curses herself for winking back.

Yeast.
Bread. Women. Beer. This is what Mark says when she tells him she might have something going on up there.

Emotions.
Not a yeast infection. The condom was defective, that Maude knows now.

God.
Maude is sure he does not exist.

Genuine human connection.

The sister of the man who died in the café explosion comes in one day and orders a London Fog. At first, Maude doesn't know who she is. She watches the woman's hand tremble as she pulls out a five-dollar bill, notices the yellow-green dried stains at the wrists of her shirt. Snot, Maude knows. She understands that natural reaction of wiping away tears and snot and horror and sadness. She tells the woman the tea is on the house. The woman confesses that her brother was an evil man—a rapist—and that it's just as well that he has blown up. Maude recalls the now-dead man and is surprised by the secrets behind tweed and sweet lemon water.

Riding off into the sunset.

Maude breaks it off with Mark. Resumes her nightly affair with Aaron Burr/Steve Buscemi. With herself, she understands.

The wonders of Japan.

While flipping through six hundred channels, Maude stops on a subtitled Japanese film. She watches it to the end. Appreciates her sister's tastes, and wishes she could tell her so.

Women in yogurt commercials.

Maude develops a mad craving for yogurt with the fruit at the bottom after watching Jamie Lee Curtis talk about the digestive benefits of yogurt during a commercial. Jamie looks so happy. Maude only wants to eat yogurt from then on. It's all her stomach can handle.

A tiny horse.

Months later, the baby begins to kick. Maude feels as if a tiny horse is living in her abdomen. She pushes back. Eventually, the baby wins.

The placenta.

They ask Maude if she wants to eat it.

M. Night Shyamalan plot twist.

She says yes.

The invisible hand.

Maude takes the baby to see her mother. The old people don't wink at her anymore. Instead, they stop her to pet the child on her softly tufted head or caress her cheeks. *She has her mother's eyes*, they say. *Yeah, she cries a lot*, Maude says—seriously, but with a smile. Her mother stops shuffling the deck and begins to build a house made of cards. Maude's daughter giggles with delight. Maude eats tuna from the can and watches as a ghost keeps the cards from falling.

Hineni

I am here. My grandmother is dead.

I like it when my gums bleed. When I spit peppermint and a string of fire-red trails in the sink. When I bruise, a yellow-gray blossom flowers beneath my skin. The blood is so close, but hidden away. I pluck and I pop and I squeeze to try and get everything out.

"What are you doing?" my husband asks. I stare into the mirror, tweezer in hand. I am plucking errant hairs. But are they unnatural? Placed there by God. Or by Mother Nature. I shouldn't even be looking in the mirror; we are sitting shiva.

My grandmother was eleven when liberated from Auschwitz. When I was eight, my parents were killed in a car accident. I went to live with my safta. When she plucked lice from my head at ten, she said the bugs had been the only thing in the camp that let her know she was alive.

Arbeit macht frei, she would say to me, when she insisted I do homework. Later I learned she co-opted the iron saying over the gates of her death camp. Work makes you free.

Nothing makes you free.

She had gone first to Israel and then to Brooklyn. Human relations were nothing like the give-and-take of a parasitic relationship, she said. She and my grandfather divorced before it was common; she left him behind in Ra'anana.

"Just tweezing," I tell my husband.

"There's nothing left to tweeze." He takes the utensil from my hand. Brushes his thumb over the bare and tender space above my eyes.

We get into bed and I feel a hair above my right eye. It's sturdy, upright and thick. I want to get out of bed and pull it out. It feels so alien there. Alone. Tomorrow is the funeral. It's only been twenty-four hours. In Jewish tradition, it all happens so quickly. My husband turns to me. Says, "Stay."

It is not long before his snores fill the air, his arm slung over my chest. I stir; he grumbles and holds me tighter. I cannot think of anything else. The hair. The foreign object. My hair. Her hair. The curls. The shaving. The lice. The sores. The moment a man tells you that you are free, but can you believe him? Is this a trick and who will watch me? I am only a child and I have no one but the parasites on my body. What will happen when I clean them away?

I fall asleep. The next morning, we say the Mourner's Kaddish, a prayer I know by heart. I see my grandmother in a picture frame. Scowling, as she did, but with light in her eyes and I think, *If she can, so can I.*

The night of my parents' funeral, she told me that the most important thing you can tell people, dead or alive, is that you are here. On this earth. To live what they could not or what they will not. *Hineni*, she said and made me say it out loud.

"Hineni," I tell the me in the mirror and I leave the single hair above my eyes where it grows.

This Is a Full-Rate Telegram

There is trouble ahead I fear STOP no don't stop I live for your knock-knock jokes under mortar fire and wonder what you are doing now STOP the barrage STOP the wailing of the children you can't imagine the sound STOP I miss Audrey is she walking now STOP tell me a story I'm listening even though I am thousands of miles away STOP they say we will get to go home soon STOP they say we will be going to CENSORED and there I will pick wildflowers for you STOP poppies STOP they talk so much about the flowers STOP know they will not last but maybe they will last longer than CENSORED STOP Marty has died Cyril Antony Judah and Benjamin too STOP tell their wives their children STOP no don't tell them STOP they will hear STOP tell me a story STOP love STOP not much longer STOP QUOTE knock knock UNQUOTE Who's there STOP

Acknowledgments

Many thanks to the readers and editors of the following journals who've published stories included in this volume: *3Elements Review, Bartleby Snopes, Bodega Magazine, Brain Child Magazine, Citron Review,* the *Compassion Anthology, Connotation Press, Duende, Fiction Southeast, Gravel, Hobart, Hypertrophic Lit, Intrinsick, Jellyfish Review, Longleaf Review, Minnesota Review, Monkeybicycle, Necessary Fiction, New Delta Review, No Tokens, Pacifica Literary Review, PANK, Paper Darts, Pidgeonholes, Roanoke Review, Storychord,* and *Whale Road Review.*

Thank you also to all the other journals and teams who have published my work. To Tin House and Writing x Writers for fostering and encouraging my work through your workshops. To Pen Parentis and Artist Trust for your support. Thank you to my writing community, here in Seattle, and around the world. To my supportive friends and family, you have no idea how grateful I am for your words and actions of encouragement. Thank you to Jesse Lee Kercheval and Brigid Pearson for creating the perfect book jacket for my stories. Thank you to Marisa Siegel, Anne Gendler, Olivia Aguilar, Mary Klein, Steve Straus, and the team at Northwestern University Press / Curbstone Books. I am honored to be on your shelf.

To anyone who is living in a world where they don't think they have a say, this is for you.